# Daulton Dickey

I0622059

Other Books by Daulton Dickey

*A Peculiar Arrangement of Atoms: Stories* (DDE Books)
*Elegiac Machinations* (Exeunt Reason Books)
*The Lost Book of the Dead: Poems (*Riot Forge)

# Daulton Dickey

Cover by Daulton Dickey *and* Alice Dickey

**www.riotforgestudios.com**

www.daultondickey.wordpress.com
www.facebook.com/ddickeywrites/

*For Jit*
*I miss you, motherfucker*

L.H.O.O.Q.

Like an explosion propelling a bullet from its chamber, Gummo's fist blasted through the air and rocketed toward me. I arched my back and punched his forearm, altering his fist's trajectory. But it was close: you could have slid a sheet of paper between the knuckle of his thumb and the underside of my chin.

—Good reflexes.

—Try that again and I'll bury you here.

—Calm down. Christ. I'm just playing.

—We have a job to do, goddamn it, and I'm not about to let you sabotage our plans.

—Your plans. He sucked something from his teeth. —I'm just here for the ride.

—He was your friend, too, you inconsiderate prick.

—And I've paid my respects.

—The hell you have.

A car alarm wailed in the parking lot.

The sounds bounced around the enclave between the lot and the front doors.

My head throbbed.

I hated car alarms.

We were standing near the entrance of a twenty-four story hotel-casino, perched on the edge of Lake Michigan.

It illuminated the night sky.

Signs glowed and sparkled.

They spat light and strobed shadows.

Gummo and I navigated around cars in the valet corridor, a strip of concrete separating the building from the parking lot—where that goddamn car bleated and wailed.

A valet attendant, dressed in red, glanced at me as he squatted into a car. He flashed an expression as if he'd smacked his thumb with a hammer.

Face pinched.

Eyes focused yet vacant.

Glass sparkled all around us.

Windows and doors shimmered, seemed to undulate, as they reflected neon light.

Music played.

The smell of cigars wafted toward us.

An air-conditioner blasted us—it was overhead, between two refrigerator-sized chandeliers. It sounded like a jet engine.

A group of women cackled as they slipped into a revolving door.

Gummo tapped my shoulder, nodded.

—I smell a distraction, he said.

—Not tonight.

—Fucking stick in the mud.

A map near the revolving door showed the hotel and riverboat, dissected, from above.

I traced the lines with my finger, trying to memorize the layout.

The lobby housed several restaurants and buffets, but the map only indicated one bar.

Two tunnels connected the hotel to the riverboat.

I hadn't known about the second tunnel, which could prove useful.

The hotel itself resembled something you'd find in Las Vegas: a spiraling tower with colored lights racing up and down its facade.

And the casino itself was a riverboat, a term used loosely.

Indiana had passed a law legalizing gambling—but not on land. So a Nevada conglomerate built a hulking box—loosely dubbed a "boat"—on Lake Michigan.

The hotel towered on the land beside it, tunnels connected both structures.

The schematics brought Legos to mind.

—The fuck are you doing? Gummo jabbed my shoulder. —Open the door already.

—You forgot the magic word.

I flung open the door and slipped into the foyer. The door sung—whoosh—as it swung back, then its breathy contralto dissolved into a staccato baritone—crack.

Gummo kicked the door and said, —You son of a bitch, as he rubbed his face.

—Clip your jaw?

—What do you think?

—That will teach you for trying to sucker punch me.

—I deserve a free one for this.

—Drop it, I said. —Let's stop fucking off and get this thing going.

—Drop it? You just hit me in the face. With a door.

—I'm not joking.

He leaned into me, grinding his teeth.

—You're lucky I'm in a forgiving mood. Prick.

He tittered and sauntered away.

For a moment, a millisecond at most, I considered shoving him. I imagined my fist plowing into him and his face slamming into the ground.

It was a beautiful image.

My muscles twitched. Every axon transmitted declaratives: 'get him get him get him.'

Not now, I thought.

Not tonight.

He circled a couple up ahead and laughed about something. Then he touched a woman's dress.

She said something, so did her man-friend.

Gummo raised both hands and said something something.

He sneered as he spoke.

I could only imagine what snark he'd blurted out.

Probably along the lines of, 'I don't know who wears the tighter panties, you or her.'

Would drugs and alcohol control or exacerbate him? Christ, what was I thinking?

My thoughts splintered and dissipated as we slid into the lobby, a vaulted-ceilinged cathedral.

A secular monument to vice.

Our kind of place.

Stained glass windows, backlit by halogens, adorned soffits below the arches. Devoid of kitsch or irony—no slot machines, no poker chips, no waitresses—the windows depicted Jesus and saints, soldiers and the American flag.

We couldn't escape such iconography. Not even here, of all places.

—The fuck does Jesus have to do with gambling? I said.

—He crapped out.

We hemorrhaged another minute or so making jokes. Then we pushed on, toward the tunnel, which reminded me of a cave as designed by Jim Henson: An O telescoped outward, bridging the hotel to the boat. Lights augmented a mosaic-carpeted floor. They dotted the walls and ceiling, the latter of which brought to mind a set of yellowed teeth.

The tunnel smelled like beer and cigarettes, cigars and popcorn.

People strolled through it.

Some happy and joking, Others dour, silent, laconic.

A room—more like a box—stood as a sort of crossroads, which branched into two tunnels.

Security guards stood at a podium between the tunnels.

Theirs was an eclectic group.

One was tall and bulky, built like a football player. The other, short and round, like a pear.

Two gray-haired women flanked their male counterparts.

They scanned everyone in the tunnel, then they settled their eyes on Gummo and me, for some reason.

A line had formed.

Gummo and I hovered near the rear.

The pear-shaped guard yawned and slapped the back of his head. Something about him, something I couldn't place, fascinated me. His arms moved in jerks, as though I were inferring movement without witnessing it.

He smirked at something, and his mustache, a bushy caterpillar, fluttered. It seemed inauthentic somehow, as if he'd purchased it at a novelty shop.

A diminutive woman at the front of the line swung back as Mustache Man snatched her driver's license.

He slid it into a slot in the podium.

The woman barked in annoyance.

Mustache Man ignored her as he pushed a button on a device—adding a digit to a running count of everyone who had passed through the tunnel.

After pulling the woman's license from the slot, he shooed her into the second tunnel, the one on the right.

He smirked at his Linebacker-sized colleague as he redistributed his weight from his right leg to his left.

Linebacker mumbled something.

Mustache Man smirked again—what was with the smirking?—and rested his hand on a bulge on his utility belt, which housed handcuffs, a can of mace, a Taser, and a two-way radio receiver.

His partners wore identical belts, and it worried me.

Brutes on the prowl, equipped with mace and Tasers.

Bad business.

Gummo cleared his throat and slid to the front of the line. He handed his license to the Linebacker and pinched it when the Linebacker tried to take it.

The Linebacker lowered his eyebrows and frowned.

No sense of humor.

He studied Gummo's license, as if deconstructing each line, decoding every word and number.

A beat.

Then he glanced at Gummo.

In response to the Linebacker's gaze, Gummo stiffened his back and angled his head, preparing for a fight.

The Linebacker puckered his mouth.

If he were intimidated, or even annoyed, he concealed it well.

Gummo shoved his license into his wallet and waited for me. He mouthed the words 'knob gobbler' while gesturing to Linebacker.

—Well? Linebacker said, to me.

After examining my license, he glanced at the ceiling.

—I know you?

—I doubt it.

—You sure?

I nodded.

His eyes widened.

—Ole boy's funeral, he said. —You were a pallbearer, right?

—Ole boy?

Acid corroded my veins.

Gummo joined me, leaned forward.

Ready to fight.

His stance, his eagerness, shook me, so I grabbed his arm and pulled him to the tunnel.

—He had a name, Gummo said, to the Linebacker. —Asshole.

—Watch your mouth.

—Respect the dead, I said.

I imagined rushing the Linebacker, removing his face, and stapling it to his ass.

The image pleased me.

Gummo said something or other but I wasn't listening.

I didn't care.

Fuck that guy.

—We could've taken him, Gummo said.

—Part of me wanted to, believe me.

—Then let's go back.

—Later.

We walked without jogging, jogged without running, and somehow blasted through the tunnel.

For some reason, a reason I couldn't comprehend, I thought of parasites tearing through an artery.

Adrenaline ignited the hemoglobin spinning through my veins.

It clouded my mind.

Entangled and disentangled my thoughts.

We reached the end of the tunnel and leaned against a handrail on a platform overlooking the boat.

Two stories deep, as large as a Vegas casino, the boat was crammed with slot machines, card tables, digital card games, and roulette wheels.

Fewer than three dozen people occupied it.

Bivouacked on both levels, men and women, young and old, camped at slot machines and card tables.

A few walked around, eyeballing games, money clutched in their fists.

—Am I hallucinating? I said.

—You'd better not be. Not without me.

—They should be busy.

—You didn't take anything without sharing, did you?

—Why is it dead?

—Because if you're tripping, I want to …

—I didn't take a fucking thing, goddamn it. Now why the fuck is it so fucking empty?

—It's still early. People will filter in and piss away their paychecks any time now.

I gestured to a woman, a man, and the vast expanse between them—a space the size of a football field. At least.

—We're fucked.

—Push come to shove, we'll make it work. Let's just find the bar.

Machines buzzed and whirred.

Music and sound effects assaulted us from every angle.

People surveyed machines.

They inspected them, tapped them or hovered their hands over them, as if trying to divine the presence of luck, or fortune.

Fortuna wouldn't give a damn about them.

Great.

Now Gummo was in my head.

Card tables and roulette wheels bookended aisles and rows of slots.

But few people occupied them.

Luck, it seemed, appeared sweeter in the form of a box feeding you music and cartoon sound effects.

—Look at this, Gummo said. —You're upset there are so few people here. Well, I'm annoyed there as so many.


The bar resembled the casino floor, only worse: three people—all old men—hunched over a western-style bar top.

A bartender leaned against a counter, flipping through a magazine.

Televisions reiterated the day's sports scores while a jukebox played an old doo-wop song.

The noises merged, sounded almost metallic.

They rocked my head.

I wanted to destroy them.

All of them.

The three drunks sat apart from each other. At least one stool separated each of them.

The bartender raised his eyes as we approached the bar, then he refocused his attention on the magazine.

A fallen needle would have startled all of them.

—Christ, Gummo said. —I hate this place already.

—Feels like they're in mourning.

—They will be, he said, laughing. —Soon enough.

—That's a little melodramatic, isn't it?

—Where's your sense of humor, man? It's been missing for weeks. I'm about ready to send out a search party to find the fucking thing.

—Fuck off.

He tittered and drifted toward the jukebox.

I fell into a barstool and popped a cigar into my mouth.

The bartender ignored me.

I patted my pockets, in search of my lighter, and waved the bartender over.

The prick thumbed through his magazine, examining its pages with empty eyes, and ignored me.

I found my lighter and blew smoke upward. It expanded and curled around a lightbulb suspended overhead. I blew more smoke. It curled, spiraled, dissolved. Then I blasted a cloud at the bartender.

Smoke engulfed him but he didn't look up.

He didn't investigate.

I leaned my chair back, shifted forward, and slapped the bar top with both hands.

—Goddamn it, I said.

He dropped the magazine and lunged forward, startled.

—What the eff, man?

—Give me a bourbon, *Jim Beam*, on the rocks. And my friend back there will have … To Gummo: —Hey, cocksucker, what do you want?

Gummo flipped through song selections on the jukebox. —Milk from your mother's tit.

—He'll have a *Jack* and *Coke*.

The bartender shifted his eyes, held his gaze on Gummo, then shifted them back to me.

His left eye, foggy and misaligned, more or less stared at his nose. His hair, greasy, stuck to his forehead. His beard, thin, like whiskers, ran alongside his jaw. The entire package brought to mind a mid-90s-era gangbanger. The style nauseated me: another white suburbanite—inspired by pop culture—had co-opted inner city culture and treated it as some sort of personal inheritance.

Christ, he bored me.

—Chop, chop. I clapped my hands.

He sneered as he spun around to mix our drinks.

Behind me, Gummo muttered expletives. Curses, obscenities, outrages and titters, followed by the meaty sound of a palm smacking metal.

—Shit, he said, as he fell into a stool beside me. —It's all pop music and shit from the 50s. Nothing in between.

—It's all noise anyway.

—Let me have one of those.

I tossed him a cigar. He torched the end, then threw my lighter at me.

The bartender returned with our drinks. He exhaled through his nose and scanned something behind us.

He didn't make eye contact with Gummo or me as he set our drinks on coasters.

We ponied up the money. In a rare move, Gummo tossed him an extra dollar.

One of the drunks swung toward us after the bartender went back to his magazine. He was an old man—his hair thin and gray, textured like hay, his skin gray, and his eyes, red-rimmed, gazed into a void behind us.

Why couldn't these people look at us?

The old man dropped his hands onto the bar and rested his chin on his hands, sighing.

He twisted his neck and furrowed his brow—as in singular: the man sported a fucking unibrow.

Gummo fitted a pair of glasses on his face. He'd found them at a thrift store and thought they were hilarious. The lenses were missing, but, in certain conditions, the light bounced off the frames and created the impression of intact lenses.

Gummo leaned into the bar, palms on the bar top, and stared at the old man, who didn't blink.

Or turn away.

Gummo curled his finger around the frame and slid it through the lens-less gate—a cheap magic trick, a gimmick he stole from some comedian.

The old man didn't blink.

—Shit, Gummo said. —Let's buy this man a drink. To me: —He should be liquored up before the violence begins. Hell, everyone should be.

—Violence? The old man's face drooped. It resembled a corpse: sunken eyes, limp flesh.

I cocked back my hand but didn't slap Gummo.

—Might as well tell him, he said.

—Feel free.

—You're the writer. Better with words and such. He wore partial dentures. They altered the phoneme 's,' transforming it into a *shhh*, an almost airy whistle.

The old man sat up, stiffened his back, dropped his hands into his lap, put them on the bar again, leaned forward, and so on.

His eyes, wide, alight with panic, bounced from Gummo to me, from me to Gummo.

I waved to the bartender. —Get this man a drink.

—Rum, the old man said. —Now what's this violence talk all about?

—Rum, I said, to the bartender. —And you'd better fill a large glass. He's going to need all the help he can get.

—For Chissakes, what're you talking about?

—It's been all over the wires. It's even been picked up nationally. I'm stunned you haven't heard about it.

**15**

—Should spend less time paying attention to sports, Gummo said.

—Reporters are swarming the area as we speak.

—To document the carnage.

—What carnage? Christ, boy, you ain't saying nothing.

—Good old-fashioned violence.

—We will soon witness, perhaps even engage in, I know I certainly will, the most brutal riot this nation has seen. In decades.

—Easily.

—Easily, I said. —Shit, I can't believe you haven't heard about it. Chaos is coalescing in your backyard, for fuck's sake, and you're oblivious.

—They're expecting thousands, Gummo said. —This town is going to burn. Tonight. And I guarantee you this place, this den of vice and desperation, will be a juicy target.

—Terrorists?

—The disenchanted, I said.

We flailed our arms as we relayed the 'news'—a performance.

The other two drunks approached us, listening, and dropped into stools beside the old man.

The bartender, still dead-eyed, sat on a chair behind the bar. He held his magazine, but his attention was on us.

Bartender: Who's expecting them?

Gummo: The Governor. He's been on top of this all day.

Me: Jesus. You mean none of you have heard about this?

They shook their heads.

Gummo: We just came from the Reserve base in LaPorte and ...

Me: The Governor himself ordered two thousand troops on standby.

First Drunk: You in the reserves?

Me: We're journalists. Here to cover the ...how should I say it? ... event.

Old Man: What event? Christ, say something.

Second Drunk: What do we need to know?

Me: Stay off the streets. You don't want to be caught in the shit when this blows into town.

Gummo: That's right. Governor's orders. Stay where you are. Don't risk leaving or going home. It's too dangerous.

Me: Just stay put.

Second Drunk: Jesus God.

Old Man: But what's going to happen?

The bartender dropped his magazine and slipped into the backroom. I nudged Gummo, gestured to the door as it closed.

—Total madness, I said, still watching the door. —Apparently a group of old school anarchists are tired of the plutocracy.

—It's going to be like the French Revolution and shit. Heads will roll.

—Christ Almighty.

—You people seriously haven't heard any of this? Gummo said.

I smacked the bar top. The second drunk flinched.

—Go outside, for fuck's sake, I said. —You can practically feel the tension in the air. How can you be so oblivious?

One of the drunks, a robust man with a shiny pate, stood and knocked on the bar.

—I got to find my niece, he said. —Make sure she gets back to her kids before this …

—No, I said. —This stays here. You stay here.

—Goddamn it, Gummo said. —Haven't you dunces heard a word we said? 'Don't risk leaving or going home.' Remember?

—That don't make sense. They trying to get us killed?

—But it does make sense, I said. —Look at it from the Governor's point of view: if these riots turn out to be rumors, he doesn't want people fired up for no reason. That might lead to a self-fulfilling prophecy. Shit, you know how people are. As groups, they're stupid and irrational. Easy to move, to push into a stampede. You spread rumors of riots, and morons and psychopaths will make sure it happens. People will get so worked up, the tension and suspense, the anxiety, will become too much to bear, and, before you know it …

—Bam, Gummo said. The drunks leaped, startled.—Anarchy, which is just what those cocksuckers want.

The bald man frowned. —Bow how in the world are we supposed to keep something like this to ourselves?

18

—Then go tell everyone, moron, and see where that leads you.

—But if you stoke the violence, I said, —or inspire it, blood will be on your hands.

—Goddamn. The world's gone crazy.

—I'll drink to that.

I swallowed my bourbon.

A man blew into the bar, flanked by two security guards. He was tall, wiry, with a face like an owl—all eyes.

And he was wearing a suit.

An executive of some sorts.

Maybe someone who could help us.

The bartender emerged from the backroom and gestured to Gummo and me. Under different circumstances, I might have called him Judas, but we had hoped someone would betray us.

—Sirs, Suit Man said. —I'm going to have to ask you to come with me.

—Get the fuck out of here, Gummo said.

—Or I can call the police.

I screwed my cigar into the ashtray, snuffing it.

Suit man cleared his throat. His security guards clenched and unclenched their fists.

—I don't know about you, I said, to Gummo, —but the second option seems more palatable.


We had followed them down a hallway, which reminded me of a hospital: sterile smell and fluorescent lights.

Suit Man stopped at a door and flung it open, gesturing for us to go inside. He paused, nodded to the security guards, who stayed outside, clicked his tongue, and closed the door behind him.

His office was white and sparsely decorated: a desk here, a chair there.

A photograph of a man wearing a cowboy hat hung beside a clock.

Suit man cleared his throat as he took his seat. He pointed to two chairs on the other side of the desk.

We stood.

—Sit.

We sat.

I clenched a cigar between my teeth and searched for my lighter, hoping I hadn't left it downstairs.

Gummo wiggled in his chair.

He pushed the glasses up the bridge of his nose and rested his hand on his face—thumb on chin, index finger on temple—and studied Suit Man's face.

—There's no smoking in here.

—Figures.

I pocketed the cigar.

—What are we doing here? Gummo said.

—Steve Myers said something about a riot?

—Who the hell is Steve Myers?

—The bartender.

—Fucking pansy.

—He should have kept that to himself.

—They don't listen.

Suit Man interlocked his fingers behind his head.

—And why is that? he said. —Why should he have kept it to himself?

We told him a variation of the story, tempering its ominousness.

—If you're supposed to cover the riot, then why here, why in my house?

—We're in your house, I said, —because, for us, the riot is incidental. Background noise, so to speak.

—How so?

—We were given this assignment weeks ago, before the rumors. If the riots happen, we're prepared for them.

—Either way, we've got a story to write, Gummo said.

—And what assignment might that be?

—A human interest thing. Fluff. About gambling and such.

—That's right. It's nonsense. More or less PR.

—So you're hoping for riots?

—It'd be more fun than interviewing old ladies, to be honest.

—Speaking of which, I said. —Our publisher said you were informed we were coming. He said you, or whomever, would comp us. A room for the weekend. Chips. For gambling. So we can get inside the story, as it were.

Suit Man laughed.

We didn't.

—This is the first I've heard of it.

I smacked the desk.

—Fucking Flanagan, Gummo said. —He said this'd been taken care of.

—I'd say you two were misinformed.

—He said he talked to whasisname? Gummo snapped his fingers. —Jim Goggle-something.

—Goggins?

—That's it. Jim Goggins.

Suit Man cleared his throat, as if to supplant either a grunt or a string of expletives, and picked up a phone.

He pushed a button and waited.

Waited.

Then he barked at someone on the other end.

A smile danced across Gummo's face.

Blood pumped through my veins. It picked up speed as it tore through my heart and rocketed back again.

For a moment, for a brief second, I allowed a smile to flutter across my lips.

We'd worked on this for weeks: manufacturing a website for an imaginary newspaper, filling it with *AP* and *Reuters* stories, stamped with our bylines. We even took pictures and interviewed a few people around town, a few business owners. Fluff pieces.

On establishing our "news organization," Gummo had called the casino, passing himself off as our publisher, and convinced Jim Goggins to provide us with money and two hotel rooms. It was a convincing performance, although the accent annoyed me: Gummo had, for reasons he never explained, affected an accent reminiscent of Jackie Mason. No kidding.

Suit man said something else and hung up.

—Goggins apparently went over my head to accommodate your paper. He rocked back and forth, back and forth. Blood rushed to his head. His face reddened. —I don't like this at all. There's something about you two ... I don't like it. Rest assured, I'm going to watch you. Closely.

—No need for that, I said. —We are professionals.

—I find that hard to believe.

Gummo laughed.

I wanted to punch him.

—Now, Suit Man said. —Tell me about this riot business.

—Probably nothing more than a rumor.

—Then why are you here?

—You don't listen, do you? Gummo said. — We told you: we're here to do a piece on the casino.

—But if the unthinkable does happen, God forbid, we'll switch our focus to management. See how you handle the ordeal.

—We're prepared for anything.

—Then my colleague and I have nothing to worry about.

Gummo glanced at me. I read concern on his face, a concern I shared. If they were prepared for "anything," then inciting a riot might prove harder than we'd hoped.

We had expected two rooms but Suit Man overrode corporate and gave us the equivalent of a walk-in closet and told us to share it. He also gave us paper vouchers guaranteeing money and one free meal each.

The comps were valued at two hundred dollars apiece—a stunning number. We'd anticipated something like fifty dollars, split between us.

—Lovely, I said.

The beds were small, somewhere between toddler and twin sized. But they called to me, somehow appealed to me, and I considered a nap. I considered lying down. I considered going over our itinerary, to reiterate our timeline.

To pound it into Gummo's skull.

We only had six hours to fulfill our objectives. Three hundred and sixty minutes until sunrise. Twenty-one thousand six hundred seconds to right wrongs, justify life, give meaning to death, and celebrate a posthumous birthday.

—Yeah yeah blah blah something something.

Gummo's rapid-fire sentences pulled me back into the real world.

He wanted to get drunk, he said.

He wanted to get fucked up.

He wanted to gamble and drink and do drugs.

And he wanted to witness chaos.

He wanted to orchestrate it.

—I'm ready to unleash some fucking anarchy already, he said. —Christ, let's go go go.

He'd recently spent five weeks in lockup, so I chalked up his energy to state-enforced cabin fever.

—Jail rotted your brain, I think.

—It reinvigorated me.

His crime was defacing private property.

A billboard.

It loomed over the main drag in town, and it had haunted and irritated us for months.

An advertisement used the *Mona Lisa* to flog health insurance, which had bothered us for three reasons: 1) *Mona Lisa* was pointless; art served no purpose if it wasn't transgressive; 2), Marketing was propaganda; it manipulated people by exploiting psychological biases; 3), health insurance assured the rich survived and the poor suffered. Together, the pastiche served as a symbol for everything wrong with our civilization: art as kitsch, marketing as religion, money as power and well-being.

We'd joked about destroying it, we'd complained whenever we passed it, but we didn't do anything.

Then one night, drunk, Gummo had scaled the billboard and, in the spirit of Marcel Duchamp, painted a mustache and goatee on the woman's face.

Below the painting, he wrote *L.H.O.O.Q.* Then he scribbled 'This is not art' across her forehead. And 'True art is not a marketing tool' over the company's logo.

—Screw waiting, he said. —You know what? Fuck gambling altogether. Let's just go down there and get crazy.

—We stick to the plan.

—This is going to rawk. A southern accent slipped into Gummo's speech whenever excitement seized him, a strange affectation because, as far as I

knew, he was born and raised in Northern Indiana.
—Fucking rawk. He punched his palm, bounced from
foot to foot.

He reminded me of Neal Cassady, for some
reason.

—I can't fucking wait, man. I'm excited. Can
you tell I'm excited?

He jumped onto a table and kicked the wall
behind him, propelling himself forward, then he hit the
bed and rolled to the floor.

Laughter.

Titters.

He threw his fists into the air as he scrambled
to his knees and shouted, —For our comrade.

—You need to calm the fuck down. We have a
long night in front of us and I don't want you blowing
a fuse this fucking early. I want you on board here.

—Inciting a riot, vandalizing a museum,
kicking some ass: how could I not be on board?

—Quit treating this like a game.

—Quit treating me like a child.

—Stop acting like one and I'll stop treating
you like one.

—If you want me to calm down, then you'll
have to pass over those drugs you're sandbagging.

—Not now.

—Give them to me.

—No.

—Yes.

—Later.

—Now.

He punched me.

The blow knocked me backward and I fell on the bed.

I bounced off the mattress and cut my chin on the nightstand.

Blood warmed my neck.

I jumped to my feet and slammed him into the wall. He fell, pulling me down with him.

He said something, swung at me, but I threw my hand out and deflected the blow, and he punched the wall.

—Get off me.

I jabbed his ribs.

He shouted 'fuck you' and threw another punch. My wrist and forearm absorbed the blow.

—You wanted to come along, I said. —Now you've got to stay focused.

—He was my friend, too. I'm part of this whether you like it or not. He lowered his head. —Just give me some of those fucking pills, man.

—They can wait.

—Just one or two. Or three. I feel like my nerves are on fire. I need them.

—You need a lobotomy.

I hit him with an uppercut.

His lip split.

Blood rolled down his chin.

Eyes wide, stunned, he tapped his mouth, examined the blood.

—Christ, motherfucker, he said. —The hell was that for?

—For sucker punching me. Asshole.

He jumped to his feet and ducked into a defensive crouch. Arms out, fingers splayed.

He spat blood and growled.

—I'm going to hurt you for that.

—Knock it off. Before someone calls management. Do you want to ground this flight before it takes off?

—I want to grind your face into the carpet.

He lunged at me. I sidestepped him and planted my foot in his crotch. He groaned and hit the floor, cupping his balls as he curled up.

—Fucker. He coughed. —Mother ...

—Keep it down.

—You just hit me in the DMZ, man.

—I said lower your voice.

—You lower yours.

I pulled a bag from my pocket.

It contained roughly three-dozen pills, each a different shape, size, and color.

I'd purchased it from a crackwhore who'd offered to blow me for three dollars.

Three fucking dollars.

The offer had sounded as appealing as paying a blind man to pierce my urethra.

She'd cocked her head to the side when I'd said that, asked if it meant 'yes.'

Maybe, I'd said, but first you need to take me to your dealer.

She refused.

He ain't no one can just walk up to, she'd said.

She pulled a freezer bag from her purse and shook it.

Pills.

What were they?

She didn't know.

How much?

Not for sale.

She needed them, she'd said. They curbed her cravings for the harder shit.

Didn't I know it'd dried up? Shit was harder to get than gold.

I'd offered two hundred dollars, a price she couldn't refuse.

A price she didn't refuse.

—Here. I tossed Gummo a maroon pill. — Now keep quiet.

—What is it?

—How the hell am I supposed to know? Just swallow the damn thing and shut your mouth.

—Give me another one.

I handed him a blue and white pill.

—That's it, I said.

I went into the bathroom to inspect my chin, dry-swallowing three pills as I crossed the threshold.

Blood drained from a quarter-sized hole.

I found gauze in a first-aid kit and taped several layers to my chin, but the tape didn't stick—too much blood was draining from the hole.

After applying enough pressure to abate the bleeding, I managed to stick the tape.

Gummo was sitting on his bed, examining his glasses, when I made my way back into the main room.

—You bent them. Prick.

—So bend them back.

—I don't want to break them.

—Then stop whining.

He twisted the frame and put on the glasses.

They sat at an angle.

—You motherfucker. These are my glasses, my Groucho glasses.

—They look fine. Now come on. Let's hit the casino before the drugs kick in.

Gummo fiddled with his glasses while we waited for the elevator. He twisted them in increments, handling them as if they were priceless heirlooms.

They unwound and settled into their now-default position.

Twisted enough to list.

—We should take the stairs.

Gummo mumbled something about complaints.

Something rose in my periphery: first a shadow, then a blur.

A woman sauntered toward us.

Seemed to float.

She watched her feet as she walked and slid a finger along the wall, skipping her hand over each door.

Petite but not tiny, curvy, slightly overweight, she reminded me of the contours of a paintbrush for some reason.

And her outfit brought bondage to mind: a vinyl top and skirt, stiletto heels, vinyl vambraces.

The outfit somehow acted as counterweight to her swaying hips.

She seemed to drift without moving her legs.

She fanned her arms out when she spotted us. Outward, inward, and outward again.

Then she fanned them toward her stomach, pantomiming a Kabuki actor exploring the aerodynamics of a paper fan.

Head lowered, chin touching her chest, she peered at us and held her gaze.

I sensed discomfort—or perhaps disgust.

She apparently shared Bettie Page's hairstylist, and so, with her head lowered, her bangs, parallel to her eyebrows, obscured her eyes.

She favored her right as she walked.

I'd dismissed the limp until she leaned against the wall and massaged her ankle.

—You okay?

She ignored me.

Gummo tittered.

She popped a cigarette into her mouth and pushed the elevator button.

—Are you going to the casino?

She hadn't looked at us. Not once.

—Here by yourself? Gummo said.

She rubbed her ankle again.

—Injure yourself?

Silence.

—We're journalists. Writing a feature on the casino. Hang with us and we can get you some comps.

—No thanks.

—Why the hell not? Gummo said. —You too good for us?

I wanted to punch him.

—Are you from the area? I said.

She held up her cigarette, studied the cherry.

—So what brings you to the armpit of America?

—Sex. Her delivery reminded me of a depressed person denying their depression: a monotone passing through barely-moving lips.

—Come again, Gummo said.

—No pun intended. I laughed.

—I was supposed to meet someone, she said. —A kid I met on the Internet. We were going to fuck.

—A kid?

—Fresh out of high school. I was supposed to pop his cherry.

—You can pop mine, Gummo said.

—You look a little old to be a virgin.

—And you look a little old to fuck teenagers.

His eyes widened.

A grin disfigured his face.

He didn't have to spin around in a panic or point out giant insects to tell me the drugs had kicked in.

His eyes, wide and vacant, telegraphed a flight from the earth to the moon.

The woman studied the numbers above the elevator. —God, she said, pushing the button again.

—I wonder if it even works.

She ground her cigarette into the carpet with her heel. —Screw this. She spun and limped down the hallway.

—We're in seven-ninety, Gummo said. —The door's always open.

She didn't look back, didn't acknowledge his invitation.

The elevators doors sighed as they opened.

—About time.

—Hey, I said, to the woman. —The elevator's here.

But she had disappeared.

—Fuck her, Gummo said.

We stepped into the elevator.

The doors closed.

Sweat poured down Gummo's face.

He turned his head—left to right, right to left, and so on—as if testing the plasticity of his neck.

His eyelids twitched.

His grin faded and reappeared.

Faded.

Reappeared.

—We should've got some cocaine, he said.

—What the hell do you know about cocaine?

—But that's why we should've done it. We should've gone all out.

—Too late now.

—Stop it. This elevator's fucking with me. I can feel … He paused, titled his head. —Can't you feel that?

He punched the wall.

—Get a grip on yourself, goddamn it. We're going into a snake pit and you're putting on blinders.

—Hear that? The world. It's humming.

—I should see a shrink for giving you those goddamn pills.

—You took them, too. Dick.

—Do you see me losing it?

He tilted his head back, wide-eyed, opened his mouth, and cackled.

—Oh, you will, mi amigo. You will.

—Like hell, I said.


A thorn bush bloomed in my skull.

Vines sprouted inside my brain.

They spread throughout my body—their thorns, razor-sharp, tore into my muscles and threatened to deglove me—as fragments of light sparkled and devoured me.

Bugs, or, worse, creatures whose existence had eluded us, crawled across my skin and burrowed into my temples. They danced and stretched a rope from temple to temple, and tried to pull them inward, tried to collapse my skull.

I wanted to scream, couldn't.

I wanted to dig my fingernails into my skull and remove them one by one.

The ropes pulled inward, inward.

I tapped my temple in search of a hole.

Gummo.

Gummo, inspect my head.

Why hadn't the words come out?

Why hadn't I made a sound?

Had my motors skills atrophied?

Where are we?

What the hell is this place?

Why the fuck are we doing this?

Although certain I'd transformed my thoughts into coherent chatter, the expressions from strangers and dealers told me otherwise. Wide or squinted eyes, open mouths or frowns—everyone broadcast a response.

Faces muted confusion or fear.

Fuck.

What had I said?

Or was it me?

Maybe they were fucked up and I was normal.

Shit.

I warned Gummo about them, told him we'd wandered into a den of freaks and deviants.

He shook his head and mumbled something about understanding.

—Something blurg blah, he said. Or seemed to: his lips hadn't moved. Or had they?

Fuck.

His eyes bulged.

Veins perforated his vitreous gel.

He laughed and jerked his head.

Sweat rained down his face. Spasms seized his arms and hands.

I viewed the world as if through a camera mounted on the back of a bee. It floated to the ceiling, then carpet, to walls, then focused on stragglers, who eyed us or thumbed their noses or ignored us.

Their faces rippled like a pond in the wake of a skipping rock.

—Everyone here is fucking crazy, Gummo said.

Lights spun, buzzers sounded, men and women flowed around us.

We paced through the bowels of some kind of beast, a monster evolved to trap people, to poison their minds.

This monster, this fucking behemoth, corrupted people, and …

Oh god, it would corrupt us, too.

And …

People watched us. Their eyes twisted and spun.

Twisted.

Spun.

Someone screamed: —Their eyes are spirals.

—Quiet down, I said. —They'll hear us.

—I didn't say anything.

—Shhh.

The monster had devoured more people. They filled rows of seats at tables and slot machines.

Aisles.

Eyeballs spun.

Faces drooped, almost melted.

People lumbered around, zombie-like.

Fuck.

Were they zombies?

Had the fucking monster killed them?

All of them?

A drunk stumbled into Gummo.

He backed away, mumbling something.

Or was he sober?

—We're in a bad place, Gummo said. —The room's closing in on us. Feel it? We shouldn't be here. This isn't worth it. Oh fuck. Jesus. Screw our homage, or whatever. Screw everything. He pointed to a wall. —Jesus Christ. Do you see that? I've got to … I must …

He stopped at a blackjack table and stared at the dealer.

She stiffened her back, glanced side to side.

Why didn't she move her fucking head?

Was she a robot?

Some sort of automaton?

Gummo leaned into me, whispered, —Look at her eyes, man. She's hatching some kind of goddamn conspiracy.

Christ.

Her eyes twirled.

Spirals.

Was she a conspirator?

No.

Stop it.

He was getting in my head, fucking with me, corrupting my mind.

I had to wrest control—from Gummo, from the drugs, from everything.

But her eyes …

Was she planning something?

But …

Stop it.

—Shut up, I said. —You'll ruin everything.

Gummo narrowed his eyes and shook his head.

Couldn't the bastard understand me?

I curled my eyebrows at the blackjack dealer, hoping to convey innocence and despair. She broke eye contact with me and thumbed a poker chip.

I tried to speak again. Neither Gummo nor the dealer seemed to understand me. Why didn't anyone understand me?

Help.

Help.

For fuck's sake, help.

The dealer glanced around the room, seeming to search for help.

Or an escape route.

—Help me, I said, shouting, —for the love of ...

My words achieved clarity. Even I sensed the distinction: they were no longer muddled or garbled.

The blackjack dealer had flinched when I shouted. She'd nearly toppled over a velvet rope quarantining the backside of the card table.

Now her eyes swirled. Then her face.

My stomach knotted.

I feigned laughter and dropped into a chair.

Her face spun, twisted, swirled.

—You should get that looked at, I said. —It could be fatal.

—Ignore him, sweeting, Gummo said, whistling as he said 'sweetie.' —He's been huffing gas.

He dropped his voucher onto the table. I clutched mine, coveting it as if Julius Caesar himself had autographed it. Gummo gritted his teeth and pried it from my hands. I sort of whined and tried to pull it away, but he yanked it from me.

The blackjack dealer held both vouchers up to the light, searching for watermarks.

Or hidden instructions?

Gummo mouthed, 'we're fucked.'

My heart raced.

But I swung my arm up and out, dismissing him.

The dealer slid the vouchers into a slot and offered something resembling a smile as she slid twenty blue and red chips across the table.

We played a hand, lost.

Played another hand.

Lost.

Another.

Lost.

—It defies logic, Gummo said.

I shushed him. He punched my arm and slapped the table and mumbled something about punishing cheaters in the Wild West.

The blackjack dealer scanned the room, her eyes searching, searching. Was she looking for the floor manager? Fuck. I was willing to wager she was looking for the floor manager.

—Ignore him, I said. —He ate some bad fish or something. I think it's gutting his brain.

Gutting his brain?

Christ, what an image.

It nauseated me.

—Come on. Fuck, Gummo said, to the dealer.
—We playing or what?

I grabbed the back of his neck and squeezed.
He arched his back, retracted his spine, and curled his
wrists and fingers—mirroring a man in a vegetative
state.

—You're going to fuck this up.

—Let go of me.

A man wearing a Hawaiian shirt took a seat
beside Gummo. A digital camera dangled from a cord
on his wrist.

—How much's the minimum? he said.

The dealer pointed to a sign. Hadn't they
programmed her to speak? The monsters.

—Oh, I guess I can swing that. Then, to me:
—Are you boys cleaning up over here?

—She's a fucking cheater, Gummo said.

Hawaiian Shirt glanced at the dealer.

—You got a wife? Gummo said. —Where is
she?

—My … wife?

—You got one?

He nodded.

—So where is she?

He pointed to a row of slot machines. —Back
there. Somewhere.

—Tell her to come over here.

—Why?

—I need someone to sit on my face.

—Hey now …

—Knock it off, I said. —I swear I'll slice off your fucking face and feed it to a paper shredder.

Christ.

Another fucked up image.

I could almost picture it.

It, too, nauseated me.

—You coward, he said. —Bring a knife, I'll bring a gun.

—I'm not kidding, Gum. If you don't shut your mouth …

He laughed. Cackled, really. Rage seized me. I grabbed a fistful of his hair and slammed his face onto the blackjack table.

The sum—his face + the table—produced an earsplitting thud, which seemed to resonate throughout the casino.

Blood had exploded from Gummo's nose. Now it expanded across his mouth and chin, a sort of liquefied Van Dyke.

—You motherfucker, he said.

Hawaiian Shirt slipped off his chair and slunk away.

Gummo wiped blood with his forearm, smearing it across his chin and cheek.

—I'll kill you, he said.

Before I could form a thought, before I could open my mouth, before I could raise my arm or stand, I watched the blackjack dealer jog to a man in a suit. She said something and pointed to us.

The man spoke into a two-way radio, eyeing us as he flapped his lips.

—Shit. See what you did?

—Me? You slammed my face into …

—We'll be lucky if they don't throw us overboard.

I jumped to my feet and grabbed Gummo's arm.

—Get the fuck off me.

—You want to go back to jail?

He wiped his mouth. Blood still drained from his nose.

—Fine. Stay here. Let this beast digest you.

I headed for the elevators, trying to regain my composure, to refrain from running, or even jogging.

Sprinting would doom me.

Two security guards rounded a corner and marched toward me.

I froze.

The elevators were at least ten yards away. The guards, five.

Shit.

Where were the exits?

Didn't this goddamn place have emergency exits?

What about fires? Catastrophes? Riots?

Fuck, I forgot about the riots.

We were supposed to incite a riot.

That was the plan.

Goddamn it.

The plan was fucked now.

Piece of shit.

The security guards neared me.

Neared me.

Why the fuck couldn't I move?

Then I saw it: a staircase.

My head floated as I spun.

I bolted.

My temples throbbed, my knees ached, my joints screamed.

Fear tore through me.

My stomach cramped and my mouth dried out.

Something behind me hissed.

A fucking snake?

Was the behemoth transforming?

Hiss.

Part of me wanted to glance at it. Another part told me not to do it.

Gummo blasted past me. He said 'shit' and fell back, running alongside me.

—You rat bastard, I said. —I hope you go down with this fucking ship.

We skipped past slot machines and people, we jumped over chairs and skidded past waitresses, we bumped into each other and leaped over a brass rail as we raced to the stairs.

Everything blurred.

The behemoth roared.

Faces swirled.

My head threatened to implode as my chest thumped, thumped, thumped.

Goddamn it.

We'd already screwed our plans.

We'd …

We blasted past a set of service elevators as the doors opened. My heart stopped. Started again. A ruckus behind us: the guards had plowed into a group of elderly women.

They slowed and attended to the women.

But one guard didn't break his stride.

—Damn it, I said.

We bolted up the stairs and raced up each story—flight after flight after flight.

Sweat covered my face and back. My calves felt as though they'd transformed into Gordian knots.

We reached the tunnel leading back to the hotel. Three guards, all brutes, flanked the O.

—What are we going to do? Gummo said.

A humming sound bloomed from the floor. I could almost see it, almost touch it. The planet was on course to a full-blown meltdown, it seemed. Or the behemoth was dying.

Either way, we were fucked.

—There's a way out, Gummo said. —It doesn't end here.

The humming sound intensified.

—Do you hear that?

Gummo closed his eyes, popped his neck. —I hear ... squawking.

—What if they have dogs? I think they're getting out the dogs.

—Or alligators. On leashes. Taught to track humans.

—We have to create a diversion. Some kind of ... Alligators?

We were ducking behind a row of slot machines, near the exit but still inside the casino. People glued to chairs pumped money and vouchers into machines. Bells rang, sirens blared, lights flickered. My mind splintered. It branched into ten thousand directions. I couldn't focus. Lights. I had to think. Blur. I needed to ... Sound effects. Needed to ...

A fire extinguisher was hanging on a nearby wall.

A guard with a 70s-era porn mustache spoke into a CB mounted on his shoulder. He paused. Listened. After a beat, he locked eyes with me and gestured to his cohorts. As if choreographed, they pushed away from their stations and marched in a V formation.

—We've got to hurry, Gummo said, —before they summon the gators.

I rushed to the fire extinguisher and tore it off the wall.

The guards had stopped maybe five feet from us.

Noise.

Shouting.

Something about dropping it.

Dropping what?

Hum.

Hums everywhere.

—Leave us alone, Gummo said. —We're innocent.

—Put down the extinguisher, Porn 'Stache said. —Now.

I blasted them.

The cloud expanded and consumed everyone.

Gummo tackled a guard to our left while I locked onto Porn 'Stache. I blasted him in the face, then I snapped a canister of mace from his belt and swung it in a wide arc as I sprayed it.

The guards coughed, rubbed their eyes.

One fell to the ground, ass in the air, howling.

Gummo cried out and dug the heels of his hands into his eyes.

I pulled him away from the cloud and dragged him through the tunnel and into the hotel corridor.

—You bastard, he said. —You blinded me.

—Keep it down.

—I can't see.

—Say another word and I'll blast you again.

—God. My eyes.

—Goddamn you, I said. —You screwed us. Our plans are fucked now.

He cackled. —That'll teach you for chattering your teeth.

Security guards blocked the entrance to the hotel lobby. Gummo and I doubled back and ran to the elevators. We took the closest one to the fifth floor, pushed the button to send it down a flight—hoping to distract our pursuers—and ran up the stairs.

My calves were on fire.

—We're almost to our room, I said. —My legs are …

—No no no. He stopped. —We can't go there.

—Why the hell not?

—Those bastards are probably already there, waiting to ambush us.

Shit.

Where were the custodial closets? Maintenance rooms?

Hotels, it occurred to me, were terrible places to hide.

A door opened and the Bettie Page lookalike peered into the hallway.

I rushed toward her, pulling Gummo behind me.

—Let us in.

—You're high.

—Look what they did to him, for Christ's sake.

—Who?

—Security. They tasered the poor bastard. Then maced him.

—What'd he do?

—Please.

—They're going to kill us, Gummo said.

She surveilled the hallway.

The elevator dinged.

Dinged.

Dinged.

—We're fucked, Gummo said.

—Please. I'm begging you.

She watched the elevator. Without moving her eyes or turning her head, she said, —All right. Get in here.


The guards thundered down the hallway.

Gummo darted into the bathroom.

**47**

Water flowed.

The sound rocked my head.

The drugs had annexed my frontal lobe and ten million million needles impaled every nerve in my body.

Lightheadedness launched my brain into the atmosphere.

Razorblades slid across my pupils as clouds slide in front of the moon.

I fell into a chair and covered my eyes.

Sweat soaked me.

My heart thumped, thumped, thumped.

The knots in my calves tautened.

Every joint and muscle ached.

Had someone dipped me in a vat of acid?

The earth manufactured sounds, ungodly noises: grinding metal, sirens, moaning corpses. Other noises I couldn't decipher or comprehend.

The bed squeaked.

It startled me.

—You okay? Bettie said.

She was sitting on the bed, inspecting me.

—You're not looking so good.

—If only you could see how I feel.

More sirens.

—The cops.

The planet screamed.

I pinched the side of my head, trying to crush my temples.

—Your pupil's are dilated, Bettie said. —Are you on something?

—Pills.

—What kind?

—Everything's strange, foreign. The world is moaning. Do you hear that? And the walls are shuddering. My back hurts.

—Sounds like acid.

—It's not acid. I think I mixed things I wasn't supposed to mix. Am I dead?

—God. I hope not. Who'd want to spend an eternity here?

—Better than nowhere.

She stared at the door as more footfalls echoed down the hallway.

—How are you getting out of here?

I tried to formulate a plan.

Tried to …

Bettie leaned back, propping her upper body on her elbows. Her hair fell over her shoulders and obscured her chest and arms. She fell onto her back and interlocked her fingers and dropped her hands onto her chest, and stared at the ceiling.

Without blinking.

Her blouse—purple satin, not vinyl, which reminded me of the inside of a coffin—was latticed in front, like a girdle.

She peeked at me, publishing something like anticipation, or expectation, in her eyes.

I wanted to touch her.

I wanted to dive into those eyes.

—Were you really going to fuck a kid?

—I guess we'll never know.

Water rumbled in the bathroom.

Was the motherfucker taking a shower?

—So … Bettie said. —How are you getting out of here?

Hell if I knew.

—Do you have a place to hide? If you manage to escape?

—We can't hide. There's too much to do. Before sunrise.

—What do you mean?

—Gummo, I said, shouting. —Are you taking a fucking bath? We've got to go.

Bettie snapped her fingers, snagging my attention.

—What do you have to do before sunrise?

—The world is our canvas. And tonight we paint our masterpiece.

—What are you talking about?

—Self-induced insanity. To honor my cousin.

—I'm sorry?

—There were a number of things we'd always discussed. Joked about, really. To Gummo: —Get the fuck out here, already. We've got to get out of here before the fucking cops show up. Then, to Bettie: —We'd always talked about scamming a casino, then … this is going to sound fucking sadistic, but … we'd always talked about trying to incite a riot.

—Jesus. What the hell for?

—Curiosity, I guess. To see how easy it would be to manipulate crowds. But dipshit in there blew it.

—I heard that, Gummo said.

He appeared in the doorway, his nose swollen and bruised.

Blood stained his suit jacket and collar.

His tie was unraveled.

—My face, he said, pointing to his nose, —is fucked, thanks to you.

—You played a part in it.

—You didn't have to bash my face into the table. Piece of shit.

—Zip it before I stomp you into the ground.

He held his arms out, as if crucified. —Come on, then, motherfucker.

I jumped to my feet.

Bettie slid off the bed and stood between us, arms outstretched.

—Okay, boys, she said. —If you start fighting, it'll be obvious to pretty much everyone where you're hiding. And I'm not going to jail over a pissing contest.

Gummo and I stared each other down.

—She's right, I said. —Sit down.

I broke my gaze and backed off.

—Make me.

I held up the mace can.

—Try it. I dare you.

Bettie put on her coat.

—Where are you going? I said.

—You mean where are 'we' going.

—Do what now? Gummo said.

—I just realized how to smuggle you out of here.

—Smuggle? Gummo tittered. Christ, I hated that sound. —How are you going to 'smuggle' us out of here?

—Where are you going next?

—I don't have to answer your questions.

—To an art gallery.

—A museum.

—Whatever. Then to the country. To burn down a tree.

—How do you burn down a tree?

—Lots of gas, Gummo said.

Bettie clapped her hands. —Sounds like fun.

—This is a two-man show.

—That's right, Gummo said, —as in me and him. So thanks but no thanks.

—If I help you assholes, then I'm most definitely tagging along.

—Like we need your help.

—Then get the hell out of my room.

—The room you rented to fuck a teenager?

—Fuck off.

Gummo headed for the door. —Go fuck yourself.

To Bettie, I said: —How can you get us out of here?

—Give me some of those pills and I'll tell you.

Bettie spoke with a lilt, like an early twentieth century intellectual, or a female William S. Burroughs.

She lamented the kid who'd stood her up as she swallowed three pills.

Men her age bored her, she'd said.

They either lacked imagination or acted like toddlers, expecting everything without doing, or wanting to do, anything.

They didn't share her predilection for disaster, as she put it.

We asked her to elaborate, to define 'disaster' in that context, but she refused.

Men, she'd said, at least those she'd known, either obsessed over their futures or lived in the moment, in an existential sense, which was great in some circumstances.

But usually they dwelled in solipsistic states.

Most men, she'd said, are either dreamers or slackers.

I agreed, although I argued that dreamers are worthwhile as long as their dreams remain abstract. Longing for an excessive salary or a luxurious lifestyle isn't a dream, I'd said—it's a chore.

Or an homage, a way to honor the dead, a way for them to live through you.

—So how do you plan on 'smuggling' us out of here? Gummo said.

—You're to the point.

—I want out of here. It's not secret. It's not safe.

—He's right. We've got to get out of here.

—All right, Bettie said. —Stay here.

She slipped into the hallway.

Gummo and I hovered near the door, our ears pressed to it.

—I'd fuck her.

—Classy.

—Like you wouldn't.

I didn't respond. He'd argue if I brought up the notion of treating women like people, not objects existing solely to soak your cock. So why bother?

—You see the way she popped those pills? And talking about disasters? She's one of us.

—I doubt it.

—I can tell.

—She seems lost.

—Lost? Like a fucking cat?

—I don't know.

—I should punch her, he said, laughing.

—Do it and I'll break your face.

—Not to hurt her. To see how she responds. To prove she's like us.

—I don't think that's a ... a hot idea ... if you want to ... get into her pants.

Cramps seized my stomach.

—Who said I wanted to get into her pants?

—You did.

—When?

—You just said you'd fuck her. About thirty seconds ago.

—Oh, yeah.

He laughed.

A wave of nausea washed over me.

My stomach rumbled.

I backed away from the door, clutching my stomach, and hunched over.

—What the hell are you doing?

—My fucking stomach.

—Can't handle your drugs?

He tittered.

I wanted to smack him whenever he did it.

—Doesn't feel like it.

—Just so you know, I'll punch you if you puke on me.

—I shouldn't have taken three.

—You'll live.

The earth rumbled and hummed.

Rumbled.

Hummed.

Something like a seismic charge shifted the ground beneath me.

—I don't like this.

Gummo tittered.

—Make that noise one more goddamn time and I'll punch you.

Sounds.

Noise.

Metal.

Squeals.

Sirens.

Explosions?

—Don't you hear that, goddamn it?

Gummo narrowed his eyes and furrowed his brows, listening.

The sounds phased in and out.

In and out.

They made listening for sounds, for footsteps in the hallway, impossible.

I steadied my breath, closed my eyes, tried to focus.

Sounds, on the other side of the door.

Sounds like …

What the fuck was that?

Footsteps?

Bodies hitting the floor?

Fuck, were they killing people?

But, no …

A fucking marching band?

An earthquake?

—I'm beginning to agree with you, Gummo said. —Maybe you shouldn't have taken three.

A skyscraper-sized tarantula screeched.

—You seriously don't hear that?

—You're fucked.

Then …

I heard it.

Clearly: footsteps.

—Listen.

—I told you, I don't hear …

The door flung open. I swung at the air. Gummo yelped.

Bettie ambled into the room, laughing at Gummo.

—You scare easily.

—I wasn't scared.

—Then what was that noise? A song?

—You're goddamn right, he said. —So what of it?

—Did you see any cops?

—Not even a security guard.

I checked my watch. We had escaped the casino five, maybe ten minutes ago.

It felt like five hours.

—They'll be here any minute, then.

—So what are we waiting for?

She grinned.

We snuck into the hallway.

My nerves coiled, uncoiled, and coiled again.

Gummo and I mimicked the band on that old *Wings* cover—hunched, constantly searching: behind us, in front of us, to our left, to our right, the floor.

Panic gripped me.

Judging by Gummo's face—wide eyes, open mouth—it took hold of him, too.

Bettie led us down two flights of stairs.

We more or less tip-toed through the hallway, which ended at a glass door.

She slid a card through a slot on the control panel. A red light turned green and a lock popped.

We entered yet another hallway.

Cream-colored.

Bland.

Air conditioners rattled.

The hallways smelled like chlorine. The stench upset my stomach.

—Where are we going?

Gummo watched the ceiling as he walked. —Feels like it's closing in on us.

—Keep it down, Bettie said.

—Where are you taking us?

—The garage. It's this way.

—Garage?

—A parking garage.

—I didn't realize they had one.

Gummo slowed.

—Something's not right.

—You're paranoid.

—You're goddamn right I am. We don't know her.

—And I don't know you, she said. —You could be rapists, for all I know.

Gummo dug his fingers into my bicep. He tried to pull me toward him.

—Ram, he said. —She's going to ... I think she's going to spring a trap on us. Don't you see? She's one of them.

Confusion furrowed Bettie's eyebrows.

—I'm going to do what now?

—Don't know, you sick fuck. Then, to me: —I was wrong, man. She's not one of us. She's not ... I don't trust her. Let's get out of here.

—We are, I said. —And she's helping us.

—No. She's onto us. She's one of them.

I pushed past him.

He grabbed my arm, jerked me back.

—Don't you see? She used a card, a security card, to get us into this place. It probably leads to a fucking holding cell or some shit.

His nonsense sliced into my brain, replaced reason with emotion.

I whistled at Bettie, who was ten or twelve paces in front of us.

—Where exactly are you taking us?

—You springing a trap, you fucking bitch?

—Hold on. Shut up. Then, to Bettie: —Where does this hallway go and why did you need a card to open the door?

She help up the card. —This is for. Patrons. Of. The. Hotel. She enunciated the last four words as if mocking a deaf person. —And that, out there, is the. Parking. Garage. Which is only for, and say it together now, people staying at the hotel.

I backhanded Gummo's shoulder. —From now on, keep your bullshit to yourself.

—What's out there? His face didn't soften. —Guards, right? They waiting to take us down?

—You bastards amaze me. I'm putting my ass on the line to help you and you're … what? … accusing me of entrapping you?

Gummo raised both arms and spun in a circle.

—The truth comes out. She's setting a fucking trap for us.

My eyes hurt. It felt as though someone had severed the tendons behind my eyeballs.

Something was wrong.

What was going on?

Bettie seemed strange, almost like a walking insect.

Had she morphed into her true self?

She glanced at me as she walked.

A smile parted her lips.

She was going to eat me, maybe devour my head as she fucked me.

Gummo backed into the wall, covered in sweat.

He flailed his arms and accused Bettie of numerous crimes—incest, bestiality, kidnapping, conspiracy.

His eyes, bloodshot, spun and swirled.

Spun and swirled.

He puckered his face and opened his mouth, ready to say something, ready to accuse her, or me, of something awful, of …

—Don't utter another fucking word, I said.
—Not one more word. You're twisting everything … I can't take it. She's one of us, goddamn it.

—She isn't. Don't you see? Can't you grasp that?

—Think about it. Just stop and think. What kind of rent-a-cop pops pills?

—Ever see *Serpico*, where they smoked those joints and shit?

—She's cool, I said. —Look at her, for fuck's sake.

Gummo glared at Bettie.

She clasped her elbows.

Silence enveloped us, the kind you sense after a firework show. Or an explosion.

—Cool cool cool, Bettie said.

She cackled.

Her eyes widened and narrowed, widened and narrowed.

—You slay … slay me, she said. —You absolutely slay me.

She spoke in a melody, with a slight British lilt. It reached a crescendo when she had stressed the third syllable of 'absolutely.'

Oh, no.

Oh, fuck.

—You don't even know know. Such a stupid word, she said, —'know.'

The drugs had kicked in.

—We've got to get moving, I said, to Gummo. —The cops will be here any minute now.

—Not with her.

—Then stay here.

Bettie chattered her teeth and gazed at the ceiling.

—We might as well save ourselves, I said. —Before he drags us down with him.

Logic had routed madness in the latest skirmish between reason and insanity, and Gummo composed himself long enough to chase us.

He hustled out of the building and caught up with us in the parking garage.

Bettie led us to her car and Gummo said something about alligators.

—Let's do this, shall we? she said. —I can't imagine the cops taking much longer to get here.

Something about Bettie's face haunted me. Her eyes, on finishing the sentence—'… much longer to get here …'—were swollen, confused, broken.

They telegraphed fury. Or heartache.

Or madness.

—Might as well get this over with, Gummo said. —But you owe me one.

—Like hell, I do.

Bettie popped the trunk.

Gummo balked. —She's crazy.

—There's a guard down there, Bettie said. —
At the exit. Ride shotgun if you're convinced he won't
recognize you.

Gummo sauntered to the car door. I grabbed
his collar.

—She's being sarcastic. Moron.

—I'm not getting in that fucking trunk.

—You don't have a choice.

—She's planning something. I can feel it.

—Get in.

—No.

—What choice do you have? Bettie said.

—We can fight our way out.

Bettie screeched.

Out of humor or concern?

—That's more than reasonable, she said. —I'm
ashamed I didn't think of it.

—We're not equipped to handle their army. I
showed him the mace can. —They'd mow us down in
seconds.

Gummo crossed his arms. His face—mouth
puckered, eyebrows curled upward—betrayed a single
emotion: fear.

—I'm not … I'm fucking claustrophobic.

I laughed.

He didn't.

—Spaces, small spaces … Jesus.

—Gum, I said. —The clock's ticking. Please.
Get in the fucking trunk.

—Fine fine fine. But you first.

Bettie swayed and shifted. She curled and uncurled her fingers. Her eyelids twitched, twitched. Sweat rolled down her face. Then something detonated in her skull and her eyes flickered and dimmed and shot to the right, then to the left.

She held out her arms.

—We've got to go, she said. —We've got to … If we stay too long … they'll catch us … and …

Jesus.

Not her, too.

—They'll mangle our hands with power tools, Gummo said.

—Oh god.

Bettie dug her nails into her legs as she scanned the parking garage.

If Gummo implanted more madness into Bettie's skull, then they'd both end up shouting nonsense while dueling invisible alligators.

One psychotic was easy to manage. Not two.

But how to handle it?

'Diplomacy'—the only word to pop into my head.

Handle it diplomatically.

So, without saying a word, I lifted Gummo and threw him into the trunk.

He flailed and twisted his spine and smacked his cheek against a tire-iron.

The fall, coupled with the blow, winded him. I exploited his inertia and leaped into the trunk. Bettie winked at me as she slammed the trunk cover.

Darkness enveloped us.

It annihilated the world.

The universe.

The drugs complimented its absoluteness: I felt trapped inside a montage sequence cut against a black title card. Sounds assaulted me. Gummo gasped, cursed. His breathing slowed. Then … footsteps on concrete. Echoes. A door closed—it sounded like thunder. The car bounced. The bottom of the trunk felt like a waterbed. More noises: the engine clicked and roared and the transmission clucked as gears shifted. Wind whistled as it blew into the trunk. Gummo moaned and mumbled something. He groaned and cursed me. The car stopped. Oh shit. Why did it stop? More noises: muted chatter. A conversation. Friendly. Ding. What the hell was that? The car jerked forward. I slid and crashed into something. Gummo? Probably not. Or maybe. He was quiet. Too quiet. I didn't like it. Was he unconscious or …

The car stopped.

I rubbed my necklace. I'd forgot about it. Somehow, it had slipped my mind.

How could I have forgotten about it?

The trunk opened.

Light spilled into it, blinding me, and I shielded my eyes with a sort of salute.

Bettie gazed down at us.

—I'm jealous, she said. —That seemed like fun.

—Then get in, Gummo said. —Take a fucking turn.

—Next time.

—Where are we? His partials slipped. It sounded as if he'd said 'whirr we?'

64

—The parking lot.

—Christ, there are cameras everywhere.

—They'll know my car, she said. —We've got to switch. One of you are going to have to come up front to show me where you're parked.

—They know your car?

I jumped out of the trunk. —I'll go.

—Bullshit.

Gummo sat up.

I shoved him back inside and slammed the trunk, laughing.

He yelled, shouted, screamed.

—Twat? I said. —I cunt hear you. I think I have an ear in-fuck-tion.

Bettie punched the trunk. —Next time you'll think twice before accusing me of something.

Gummo punched and kicked the trunk.

—Oh god. Fuck. No. Run, I said, shouting. I slammed the passenger door and shouted, —Jesus Christ, what is that?

Bettie put the car in gear and eased her foot off the brake pedal.

I glanced around, searching for cops.

For security guards.

For anything.

—This isn't right.

—It is strange, she said.

—Convenient.

—So where are you parked?

—Over there.

—Where? There?

—Yeah.

—Across the street?

—We thought it was better to park there.

I tried to picture the parking lot from above. Did it look like a maze? A web of cars and concrete, aluminum posts and metal gates, all following a pattern hard to discern from ground level.

Bettie snorted. She laughed harder, snorted again, and covered her mouth.

Me: Something funny?

Her [*cackling*]: I can't stop laughing.

Me [*laughing*]: You're stoned.

Her: Really? I. Did not. Know. That.

She snort-laughed again.

Me: Our car's over there. The gray one.

Her: Which one?

Me: The only gray car over there.

I pointed to it. She snorted.

Me [*after a beat*]: You know, it just occurred to me: I don't even know your name.

Her [*shrugging*]: My name's my name. It's neither original nor endearing.

Me: Oh, now you've got to tell me.

Her: Pretend I don't have one. Pretend I'm nameless. And so it's up to you to name me.

Me: I actually thought you looked like Bettie Page, but I'd prefer to know your real name.

Her: Bettie it is, then.

Me [*laughing*]: You want me to call you Bettie?

Her: You can call me Al, for all I care.

Me: I'd rather call you Bettie.

Her: Great. Then it's settled. Now what am I supposed to call you?

Me: Ram.

Her: Ram?

Me: Ram.

Her: As in battering—?

Me: As in Rimbaud.

Her: The poet?

Me: You've heard of him.

Her: 'I have dreamed of the green night of the dazzled snows/ the kiss rising slowly to the eyes of the seas/ the circulation of undreamed-of saps/ and the yellow-blue awakenings of singing phosphorus.'

Me: I'm impressed.

Her: Why? Because I'm a woman? I wouldn't know such things?

Me: Because few people read poetry.

Her: You know, I think it's actually pronounced R*em*-baud.

Me: I prefer Ram. Rem's one step away from rim, which is another step away from rim-job, a connection Gummo wouldn't fail to make. And exploit. Endlessly.

She laughed. And snorted. And laughed again.

Her: So what's your real name?

Me: It's a need-to-know kind of thing.

Her: Let me guess: I don't need to know.

Me: Something like that.

Her: So we both have secrets. I'm okay with that.

She pulled up beside my car. I got out. Bettie pulled the keys from the ignition and headed for the trunk.

Gummo was still pouncing, still screaming.

—I dread this, she said.

—He'll whine, maybe throw a punch or two, but he'll get over it.

She popped the trunk and stepped back.

Gummo flew out of the shadows.

He tucked and rolled when he hit the ground and jumped to his feet—in a single motion.

He grunted and stomped toward me.

I tore the mace can from my pocket and sprayed him.

He howled and covered his face and fell to the ground.

Bettie waved away rogue particles. She coughed and hocked up phlegm.

I tasted it, too.

It burned like a motherfucker.

The cloud wafted toward Bettie. She jumped back, kicking her heel upward, and jabbed Gummo's jaw. He fell onto his stomach and twisted away from her.

—Goddamn, he said. —I'll fucking skin you for that.

—I'll cut off your balls and shove them in your mouth.

—Get in the car, I said, aiming the mace can at him.

—My eyes. My ... You bastard.

He lumbered to the car, nearly tripped as he opened the back door. Then, saying something or other, he fell into the backseat.

Images rocketed in and out of my mind, faint but clear: Jacob alive, laughing.

Jacob dead, rotting.

His flesh decaying, turning to dust.

Lying in a box in darkness, burns covering him.

Jacob talking.

He and I hanging out, joking.

Jacob, dead, gone, no longer able to talk or laugh, dream or fear, joke or harass.

No longer able to indulge our eccentricities.

Stop.

Get the fuck out my head.

Another image, a memory: He had called me a week before he died. He and his on-again-off-again girlfriend were fighting. Again. He invited me to go fishing. I laughed. Two modern day Dadaists fishing. What a hoot.

—But what if we turned it into a surreal outing? he said.

—Like tying toilet paper rolls to fishhooks?

—Or going to the lake in our bathrobes, throwing the rods into the lake, and swimming out to get them.

I agreed to go under those terms.

We visited a thrift shop and rounded up supplies: a powder-blue tuxedo, an oversized foam cowboy hat, used SCUBA outfit, complete with flippers, mask, and tank, although, sadly, the tank was empty. We also bought a random assortment of products, such as crutches, tennis shoes, and paperback books, videotapes and lampshades and salt and pepper shakers.

Then we decided to visit the second most populace lake in Northern Indiana.

—If we're going to act like freaks, Jacob said. —We might as well have an audience.

The lake covered nearly forty acres near the Indiana/Michigan border. Men and women and children flocked there on the weekends. Some to drink and barbecue, others to pass their time fishing.

It was one of those locations locals, especially our age, tended to avoid. Most of us treated it as the social equivalent to receiving a suspension from school because head lice had colonized your scalp. A single whisper among your peers, a rumor even, and you'd transform into a leper.

Simple mathematics defined everyone's attitude: you + kitsch = ostracization.

And the lake was kitschy.

A local artist had revived it in the late 60's—in a coup, some said.

In reality, it was nothing more than a publicity stunt meant to attract tourists.

The lake was shaped like a jelly bean. Trees encircled it: they followed an almost indescribable pattern but aerial photographs showed they encircled the lake in a Milky Way-like spiral.

Stone blocks and picnic tables filled the gaps between the trees.

A stone staircase grew out of the northernmost mouth of the lake.

It raised two stories, then plateau'd.

In other words, it was the perfect location for a surrealist shindig.

We parked near the road and hiked to the lake.

Jacob was wearing his SCUBA gear.

His signature piece, a Dali-esque melting clock necklace, dangled from his neck.

I was wearing the tuxedo and cowboy hat.

I moaned as I walked, eyes wide and mouth open, like RP McMurphy at the end of *Cuckoo's Nest*.

We carried our gear—fishing rods and props— in duffel bags and mumbled about the hell we'd witnessed in 'Nam.

Reactions to our shindigs, as we called them, never failed to amuse us.

Few people gawked, few giggled, usually children, but most either ignored us or tried to look at us without appearing interested—like viewing something out of the corner of your eye.

It fascinated me.

If you went to church in a t-shirt, people balked. But if you dressed and acted like a freak, a weirdo, they tended to overlook you. If they did talk to you, they'd stare directly into your eyes without attempting to take in the full package, so to speak.

On those occasions, we'd up the ante: we'd utter glossolalia or pretend to suffer from echolalia, or we'd flail our arms or legs or spew obscenities.

Anything to elicit a response.

Or a reaction.

Several children giggled as we approached the bank.

Families and fishermen stood in clusters.

Monofilament sparkled.

I tipped my foam hat as I passed a few kids.

They covered their mouths and giggled.

We found a vacant spot near a shade—about three feet from it—and dug through the duffel bags.

He and I had invented a language, something like a cross between Pig Latin and gibberish. We 'spoke' it while attaching Christmas tree ornaments or paper to hooks, which we cast into the water.

As buoys, paper failed.

Obviously.

But we made a game of casting our lines and predicting where the paper might land.

Ornaments only functioned as floaters about half the time.

Some floated, some dove straight to the bottom, and others broke from the hooks and drifted downstream.

Men and women laughed and joked.

They paid attention to us, sometimes ignoring their lines.

But our act bored them after a while, and they ignored us.

So we removed the more ridiculous articles of clothing and stopped speaking gibberish—although we still cast objects into the water and, on occasion, complained about nascent fish.

Jacob talked about his girlfriend.

Our antics, he'd said, had strained their relationship. She was sick of the Dadaism, of the surrealism, of the violence, and the antics.

He didn't know what to do: he enjoyed these outings, but he loved her and he wanted to keep her happy, content, satisfied.

—So dump her.

—It's that easy, isn't it?

—In this case, it is.

—I like her, Ram. I love her.

—So, what, then? You like this woman. Understood. But she doesn't like you, who you are. She likes the Jacob she imagines she can help you become.

He didn't say anything.

—You'd like that, wouldn't you? To become her ideal Jacob?

He kicked a pebble.

—Jesus, I said.

—This seems silly lately, acting like this. What's the point?

—There is no point.

—But it's getting old.

—She has you under control, doesn't she? I mean, why can't you do both? Why is it either A or B but not both A and B?

—Aren't you sick of acting like this? Getting into fights or getting so blasted you can't remember what day it is?

—We are freaks. That's the secret to our success.

—What success? We're poor and have no future. This isn't a job. It's not a career. We can't retire on memories or anecdotes. I want more. I want to do things.

—Like what?

—I want a life. A real life. I'm sick … aren't you sick of working dead-end jobs, of constantly worrying about money?

—I don't worry about money.

—Then you're the only broke motherfucker on the planet who doesn't.

—Why would I? If you don't worry, you're not miserable.

—You're the most miserable person I know.

—I'm not miserable.

—It seems to me, it's always seemed to me, that your insistence on acting out is proportional to your misery.

—I didn't realize you had a doctorate in psychobabble.

—Do you remember when Sara left?

—I kicked her ass into the mass grave of assholes I never want to think about again. Thanks, by the way, for exhuming that corpse.

—You almost convinced Gummo and me to start a riot.

—And we would have succeeded if you weren't pussies.

—A riot, for fuck's sake.

—It was your idea.

—I came up with it when I was nineteen. Nineteen. We all say stupid shit at that age.

—But your idea would have worked. I've always said that. And I'll do it eventually, manipulate a mob. And you'll be there. You may say no now, but I know you, man: you can't avoid chaos. You've never been able to.

—I've always been able to. I chose not to. But now I feel … I don't know … like I'm trapped. And I don't like this feeling.

—So what then? Pop on a suit, work in a cubicle until you're senile?

—If they pay well, sure.

—My god. What has she done to you?

—Nothing, you misogynist dick.

—I'm not a misogynist. But I am opposed to tyranny. And the control she's exerting …

—It's not her. It's me. Don't you get that? I want more than what I have. I want a house, a new car. I've never owned a new car.

—Those are delusions. Implanted by our culture.

—They're ambitions.

—But they're unnecessary. If you get a job and buy these things, you'll end up working more to pay for them, and working more and more, and you'll eventually find you won't have time to enjoy the things you're working to afford. Things you can't afford and don't need. Things that will plunge you into debt, a debt that will come back to haunt you. Then you'll work without having anything. It's a vicious cycle. You should know that. Look at your family. Hell, look at mine. I didn't have shit growing up.

—And you hate everyone who manages to afford nice things.

—I don't care if the rich have everything and the poor have nothing. I only piss on the pricks who think they're untouchable or infallible because they own a fucking house or car.

He laughed. —You're a walking contradiction. You complain nonstop about corporations and 'fat faced' businessmen.

—Not because they're wealthy. I despise them because their milquetoast, friendly-to-all-demographics are stripping us of our culture.

—Same difference.

—Huge difference.

He reeled in his line and threw it out again.

—Look, I said. —Do those things. No one's going to stop you. But don't do them, avoid those fucking dreams, and they are dreams, if you think they'll somehow make you happy. If you think they'll vaccinate your brain and prevent it from coughing up weird thoughts, from viewing the world through a skewed lens, know this: you'll never succeed. And you'll be miserable, but then you'll be too deluded to realize it.

Jacob's line snagged, entangled on seaweed. He freed the line and, dropping the rod, sat beside me and offered me a cigar.

—I can't stand those, I said. —Where are my cigarettes? Shit. Where'd they go?

He lit his cigar.

Then he unlatched the Dali necklace and tossed it to me.

—I'm not taking that.

I tossed it to him.

He dropped it.

—It's time to grow up, he said. —It's time to want something, to believe in something.

—I believe in plenty.

—In what? Yourself? Being weird?

—I believe in you, I said. —And Gummo. Beyond that, everything is …

—I know, he said. —Bullshit.

—Superfluous.

The necklace splintered sunlight.

—You're too serious too often. I stood. —Now excuse me while I go dry hump a tree.

We were racing down a road in the middle of the country when the headlights went out.

Darkness engulfed us.

Streetlights didn't exist there, not in a cornfield with a street parting it.

I'd glanced at the speedometer a millisecond before the interior and exterior lights had failed us.

The transition from light to darkness burned the number 90 into my retinas.

Bettie laughed when the lights had vanished.

The end was nigh, she said.

Gummo was lying on the backseat. He sat upright and leaned between the two front seats and said, —Blow a fuse?

—Looks like it.

—It's my dark mistress, Fortuna, he said. —She's paying you back for spraying me with mace. You're about to learn a hard lesson, mi amigo.

—You're a terrible augur. She's paying you back for botching our casino operation.

—You botched it, genius. By slamming my face into that table. Remember? Or did your battered brain already delete that?

—I was trying to calm your ass down.

Bettie cackled the way you might imagine a banshee would scream.

—'Botched our casino operation,' she said. —You sound like mobsters.

—Maybe we are.

She laughed harder.

—Apologize, Gummo said, to me, —and I won't bring it up again.

—You smoking crack back there? I'm not apologizing.

—Then may Fortuna have mercy on you. He fell back, then flung forward. —And give me that mace.

Bettie perched her feet on the seat and bent her knees, pulling them to her chest. She curled her hand around her eyes—the way a child might pretend to use binoculars—and scanned the vacuum beyond the windshield.

—This isn't funny anymore, she said. —We're going to … we're going to get into a fucking accident.

She was right.

You couldn't see beyond the hood.

Gummo jabbed the back of Bettie's neck and said, —You wouldn't believe how many sharp turns and ditches are out here.

—That's not funny.

Laughter brewed inside me.

I tried to fight it, tried hard to push it down, to stop it—but I failed.

Gummo joined me in laughing and slapped my shoulder. Through the rearview mirror I saw dried blood caked to his face. His eyes were puffy and swollen. A bruise covered the bridge of his nose and part of his cheek—it appeared as though someone had dabbed a brush in purple paint and slapped his face with it.

I held my hand over my shoulder.

—I guess I got out of hand back there.

He shook it. Then he slapped my face.

—I don't do mushy, he said.

—Guys guys guys, Bettie said. —This would be touching and all if we weren't. On the verge. Of fucking death.

—I know these roads well. I grew up around here.

—We used to come back here to smoke pot when we were teenagers. It was perfect. Dark. No cops.

—Maybe we should find a road with streetlights.

—There aren't any. Not back here.

—Hurry, then, and get us to wherever the hell we're going. She paused. —Where are we going? To that tree you talked about?

—We've a few things to do first, Gummo said.

—Like what?

The dome lights flickered.

Flickered.

The headlights fired up.

Bettie yelled, —Thank god.

—Damn it, Gummo said. —I was hoping we'd tear through the country blindfolded.

Bettie lowered her eyebrows and curled her upper lip, clearly not amused.

Gummo spun and lowered a padded leather hatch leading to the trunk.

I watched through the mirror, trying to discern his motivation.

Then it occurred to me: the booze.

We'd stored two cases of *Jim Beam* in the trunk. It was Jacob's favorite drink. When introduced to strangers, he often gave his name as Jim Beam or JB.

Gummo backed out of the trunk. He muttered something about small space and passed a bottle to me.

—Salute. He drank, took a deep breath, — Goes down smooth, and coughed.

I handed my bottle to Bettie, asked her to open it. She smelled it when she unscrewed the cap.

Why do people smell booze?

It hit me the way a burning torch might hit fire eaters: my throat and chest burned. Coughing, I offered Bettie the bottle. She waved it away.

—I'll pass.

—What's that shit? Gummo said. —You'll pass. There's no passing here.

—I loathe bourbon.

—Bourbon is amazing. Now drink up.

—Those pills twisted my brain into a knot. I don't want to mix them with alcohol.

—They don't last long, I said. —I haven't felt them in a while.

—Speaking of which, why don't you pass that bag back here?

—This is as quiet as we've been for days. Let's enjoy it.

—We have been out of control lately.

He tittered.

—People cope differently, Bettie said. —Some cry, some shut down, some find Jesus. And some try to incite a riot.

We laughed.

Then ...

Bettie formed the shape of a consonant with her lips. Something somewhere outside had snatched her attention. She swallowed the word and yelled something like 'cookout.'

And that's when I saw it:

We were racing toward a fucking tree.

A house-sized tree lay in the middle of the road. Leaves surrounded it, blood splattered around a twisted corpse.

We were seconds away from smashing into it until Bettie yelled.

I thrust both feet at the brake pedal and jerked the wheel to the right. The car spun, the tires screeched. I forced a hard left, avoiding the tree, and we launched over an incline and landed in a cornfield.

Cornstalks pounded and scraped the car.

Gummo yelled.

Bettie shrieked and curled into a ball, covering her face.

I jerked the wheel, forced a sharp turn.

The hard right had thrown Gummo around in the backseat. He grunted and moaned as he tried to sit up.

I stomped the brake pedal, spun the wheel, and plowed my foot into the gas pedal.

Sweat bubbled out of my hairline and rained down my forehead.

We rocketed forward and jumped a ditch.

Counter measures—turning the wheel left, then right—spun it in a series of U-shapes. From above, I imagined the trajectory resembled an infinity symbol.

We slid sideways.

Hitting the brakes didn't help.

Spinning the wheel didn't help.

We slid toward the tree and stopped, parallel to it.

Silence.

Time slowed.

The sounds of the world drifted, drifted, drifted.

Silence.

Was the radio playing earlier?

Silence.

Was anyone breathing?

Silence.

Then the sounds roared back.

—Everyone okay? Gummo said.

Bettie shielded her face with her hands. She didn't move.

—Huh?

—I'm fine.

—Hey, Gummo said, to me. —You all right?

The tree was old. Its bark, gray and wilted.

Dead.

Death.

Jacob.

—Ram?

—Are you all right? Bettie said.

She tapped my forearm. Her touch burned.

My hands trembled.

My eyes burned.

A tingling sensation rippled through me, as if a Venice flytrap had sprouted in my abdomen and gnawed on my sternum.

The world roared.

Sounds like screams.

Screams.

Crashing noises, like metal falling from the sky.

My hands trembled.

**83**

Trembled.

Eyes burned.

Sensation tore through my chest.

A Venice flytrap.

Gnawed on my sternum, my temples, my skull.

I popped the trunk and tried to open my door. It hit the tree. I rolled down my window and climbed out and ran to the trunk.

I grabbed a tire-iron and bolted to the tree.

—Motherfucking piece of shit.

I smashed it, beat it, kicked it, cursed it.

My muscles ached.

My legs tensed.

I swung the tire-iron until my biceps cramped, then I dropped to my knees and struggled to breathe.

Bettie and Gummo had got out of the car at some point, they stood in front of the headlights at some point, and now shadows spiraled across the ground and merged near my leg.

—We should burn every fucking tree out here, I said.

Gummo propped his foot on a branch and leaned into it.

—What are the chances, do you think?

—Tonight's been a fucking disaster. We should just get to that goddamn tree and burn it to the ground.

—Not now. We still have too much to do. Remember? Our plans and all that?

—Nothing's gone our way, I said. —Not a fucking thing.

Bettie vacillated between staring at the car and the tree, the car and the tree.

She opened her mouth and rubbed her chest.

She snorted.

She cupped her mouth and snorted.

And then she spit out the kind of laughter you'd hear at a British farce—loud and sustained.

I felt the urge to scream at her.

Gummo, too, glanced at the car and the tree. At me. A smile crept along his face. He backed away from the tree and tittered.

Christ, how that sound annoyed me.

Their laughter resonated, switched keys, seemed to harmonize.

—Explain to me what's so goddamn funny? I said.

—This ... Gummo gestured to the cornfield, then the tree. —It's ... I don't know ... funny yet grotesque. Like a dead baby joke.

—Driving off the road, hitting a tree ... that's funny to you?

—We're out to kill a tree and a tree almost killed us.

They laughed harder.

—Hilarious.

I tossed the tire-iron into the backseat and climbed in through the window. The *Jim Beam* bottle was on the floor, near the brake pedal. I scooped it up, popped several pills, and chugged the bourbon.

—What do you think you're doing?

—Calm is overrated, I said. —It's time to amp things up.

Imagine sleeping.

Or trying to sleep.

Or lying in that state between sleeping and awake, a sort of light REM sleep.

Then imagine your phone rings.

Or someone pounds on the door.

You lie in bed for a moment, wondering who the hell's bothering you.

Or maybe you know who it is.

Maybe you don't want to answer the phone—or the door—and so you lie in bed.

Then, perhaps out of curiosity, you leap out of bed and grab the phone, or open the door.

Now imagine your cousin Rodney.

He wants your help.

Go into town with him and bail out his son, your second cousin.

Was it even possible to bail someone out at three in the morning?

Imagine thinking it over.

Or acquiescing and throwing on your clothes and shoes, grabbing your keys and wallet. Half asleep, maybe, you say you'll go, but you don't feel like driving.

You're in the passenger seat now.

Racing down a county road.

No streetlights.

It's dark.

You're still trying to wake up, maybe. Rodney talks, spews the type of bullshit he's known for spewing.

Maybe you listen, maybe you don't.

Maybe you regret agreeing to this, maybe you're happy to help.

But why'd you agree to do it?

At three o'clock in the fucking morning.

Rodney's racing to town.

To bail out his son, his worthless son.

You're going faster, faster.

Faster.

Faster.

No streetlights.

Winding roads.

Ditches.

Fields and trees.

Then imagine the car jerking, maybe.

Try to imagine screeching tires.

What would it feel like to spin into a field and slam into a tree?

Picture fire erupting.

Picture it engulfing the motor, the engine.

You feel the fire beneath the car.

You see the fire inside the car.

The windows blacken.

Smoke fills the cabin.

Your seatbelt sticks.

The door won't open.

You're panicked now.

Screaming.

Or do you scream?

Are you even conscious?

Did the universe blink out on impact?

Do you suffer?

Hopefully you don't suffer.

You probably don't suffer as you burn.

Hopefully.

Why'd you agree to go?

Couldn't you smell the alcohol on Rodney's breath?

Why the fuck did you agree to go, Jacob?

Why didn't you stay in bed?

Why?

Fuck Rodney.

Fuck Rodney and his worthless son.

Fuck everyone.

Fuck the universe and everything in it.

Thoughts like those had killed my sleep.

For months.

Thoughts like those, trying to imagine the moment of Jacob's death, trying to picture what it was like to blink out of existence, had emptied my stomach on more than one occasion.

Somewhere between hitting the ditch and nearly hitting the tree, the hood had accordioned. It resembled a bent playing card lying on a pile of flat cards. My side of the car was dented and scraped, but the door opened. The frame, it seemed, had escaped damage. I was afraid the car wouldn't start but it turned over on the first attempt.

It was the first reprieve Fortuna had bestowed on us.

Gummo drove.

Adrenaline coursed through me.

I trembled.

Rage filled me and I'd intermittently blurt out curse words—or feel on the verge of crying.

Not the best frame of mind to drive, Gummo reasoned, which was valid, so I let him drive.

I lounged in the backseat and tried to stop thinking about Jacob, tried to stop imagining his final moments.

Tried to stop thinking altogether.

To everyone's surprised, Gummo drove with caution.

Not his *modus operandi.*

He wouldn't admit it but the incident had rattled him. He slid his hands along the steering wheel and shifted in his seat, back and forth, left and right. Anxiety had settled in, it seemed.

Bettie neither spoke nor glanced at Gummo or me.

What was going through her mind?

Probably regret.

Probably something like 'why am I with these lunatics?'

Without a word, without a warning, she climbed over the seat and fell into my lap. Her knee clipped my scrotum. I sprung up, cupped my balls, and groaned.

—Sorry sorry sorry, she said.

She slid into the seat beside me, snapped on her seatbelt, and scooped up Gummo's bottle of *JB*.

Her lips moved as she read the label.

She whispered something.

About some asshole.

She offered me the bottle.

I refused.

—Suit yourself. She took a long pull, made a face like someone had kicked her pussy.

—Thought you loathed bourbon.

—I'll try anything once.

A riposte, rife with sexual innuendo, leapt into my head, but I suppressed it.

—How's your head? Are the pills still …

—I don't feel nearly as bad as I did a few minutes ago.

—That's not good, I said. —You need more.

—I'll stick to the booze. Thanks.

—Later, then.

—Maybe.

She took another drink, a longer drink. Then she touched her chin to her chest, shook her head.

Gasped.

—What's your name?

—Ram.

—No. Your name. Your real name.

—It's not important.

—You know, she said. Then, in a poor German accent: —I have ways to make you talk.

—That so?

—You will suffer Herr Ram.

—I'm not opposed to suffering.

—And suffer you will. Still with the German accent. —Suffer you will.

She took another drink and passed the bottle to me.

I hit it and handed it back.

Our legs touched.

I scooted toward the door.

She slid closer, closer, and draped her hand over my knee.

Chills cooled me.

I lifted her hand and set it on her lap.

—I get it, she said. —You're gay. I'm cool with that.

—I'm not gay.

—Then you don't like me.

—You're drunk. And stoned.

—So you're chivalrous.

—I'm not a pig.

—I'm not that stoned.

—Stoned is stoned.

She dropped her hand into my lap and curled it, brushing my crotch with her fingers.

—Stoned isn't stoned, she said. —I'm not stoned.

I set her hand in her lap.

—Not now, I said. —Not tonight. And especially not if you're fucked up.

—What the hell are you two whispering about back there? Gummo said. —You'd better not be talking about me.

—Pay attention to the road.

—You were, weren't you, goddamn it?

—Quit being paranoid.

—Then stop talking about me.

—No one was talking about you, Bettie said.

She whispered something in my ear.

Gibberish.

—What was that? Gummo said. —I heard that. What the fuck did you just say?

She whispered in my ear again.

—What in God's nutsack did you just fucking say?

—Nothing, I said. —Don't worry about it.

—Fuck off, if you're talking about me.

Bettie whispered again, muttering 'gumbo.'

—I swear to Fortuna, to Zeus, to …

—Pay attention to the goddamn road, I said.

He grunted and cranked up the stereo. Rap-metal shook the windows.

—Turn that shit down, I said, yelling.

He turned it up.

Louder.

Louder.

Louder.

The music bore into my skull.

Singers and rappers complained about their lives.

I hated it.

All of it.

Music was no longer universal. It was individual, solipsistic, relegated to the lives of the singers and songwriters.

Nothing annoyed me more than twenty-something millionaire celebrities complaining about their lives while appealing to the lower and middle classes.

'You're barely scraping by. I have everything you don't, yet my life sucks. Boo fucking hoo.'

American culture was a joke. Pop culture, a marketing tool. Sucker people into adoring a product, a brand, and sell them shit. Persuade them they need something, then offer what you've told them they need.

And it was all gobbledygook.

You could describe this generation's quote unquote artists with adjectives such as 'trite,' 'meaningless,' 'solipsistic,' 'forgettable,' 'uninspired.'

Insignificant.

Disposable.

Transgressive artists, surrealists, or anti-artists producing nonsense—the only people worth admiring.

Corporations had facilitated the obsolescence of art—true art—through marketing strategies, studies of demographics, mass appeal.

Stockholders now defined 'art.'

Record labels and movie studios, literary agents and publishing houses employed former shoe or cereal executives to oversee the production of easy-to-market—and instantly forgettable—rubbish.

Art, true art, didn't mean anything.

Not anymore.

Gummo was right: it was a marketing tool, something you either used to market a product, or it was a product you marketed.

To a broad audience.

And by doing so, you stripped it of depth, importance, meaning.

Everything was all-inclusive and inoffensive.

Nothing mainstream challenged anyone.

You couldn't challenge audiences.

You couldn't use polysyllabic words because, by doing so, you appeared to condescend to people too lazy to pick up a dictionary. And in our anti-intellectual culture, you were ridiculed as 'elitist' if you understood concepts too dense or complicated to comprehend.

Movies: mindless.

Music: mindless.

Literature: formulaic middle-class nonsense.

No one in the mainstream took chances.

Publishers steered clear of anything outside the norm, or anything too radical or 'offensive.'

If they couldn't market it, then they wouldn't publish it, so they sought clones of successful novels, which they could market.

Just sell it to the same people who bought the book this one or that one mimicked.

Brain dead monkeys apparently ran marketing departments for publishing houses.

Art itself, modern art: nonsense masquerading as philosophy.

Cold war propaganda, sold to the masses, who inherited it without understanding its origins.

Modern art: a commodity, an investment.

Or something meant to impress, not to change minds or perceptions.

Corporations had ground culture and art into dust and sprinkled it into the eyes and ears of any moron willing to exchange time or money for mindless entertainment.

And our culture suffered.

Society suffered.

Our willingness to consume the same products, our willingness to conform to similar tastes was more than homogeneity—it was setting us up for totalitarianism: collective taste replaced individual flavor.

True individuality only lasted as long as marketing departments overlooked it.

Then it vanished when they set their sights on it.

For more, see Dadaism, Surrealism, the Beats, Grunge, Hip-Hop.

Eager to exploit the latest fad, or the latest underground movement, they assimilated it, copied it, sold it through 'hip' and 'edgy' marketing campaigns.

And the masses loved it.

They anesthetized themselves with the intellectual equivalent to snake oil while priding themselves on corporate and political propaganda: You are an individual.

You are an individual.

You.

Individual.

Yet they criticized Gummo and Jacob and me for acting like freaks, for occasionally wearing mascara and throwing ourselves down staircases, for failing to succumb to fad after fad, for living our lives as we chose to live them: free from the pressures of mass produced pyrite.

Sure, we bought into it when we were younger—almost everyone did—but we outgrew it.

At least Jacob and I did.

Gummo, however, still embraced aspects of it.

Like that goddamn rap-metal.

—Please, I said. —That shit's going to give me an aneurysm.

Gummo turned down the music. —Had enough? But he didn't turn off the radio.

—Where were you? Bettie said. —Just now?

—Nowhere.

—What's on your mind?

—Nothing.

She cupped my knee again.

I pushed her hand away.

—So it's me.

—It's not.

—I can tell.

—One, tonight is too important to get sidetracked. Two, we're both fucked up. Three, I just got out of an awful relationship, and I refuse to so much as think about it, and …

—Welcome to the club.

—So you understand.

—If I were courting you, yeah. I'd understand. But I'm not proposing marriage. I just want to have fun. With you.

Christ, she resembled Bettie Page. The words 'spitting' and 'image' came to mind.

I'd developed a crush on Bettie Page in my preteens—and it lasted for years, until I realized the images themselves were marketing tools for the retro pin-up lifestyle.

Still …

Bettie was gorgeous.

But …

No.

Stay focused.

You have to say focused.

I tapped Gummo's shoulder. —Give me the pills.

—What? He glanced back at me, jerking the wheel as he turned, and the car swerved.

I punched his shoulder, gestured to the road.

—I meant to do that, he said.

—Give me the bag.

—How much money you got?

I pulled the mace can from my pocket and held it up.

—Do you want another facial? Now hand it over.

—You wouldn't. Not while I'm driving.

I pointed the nozzle at him.

He stiffened his neck and shouted —Okay okay okay, and tossed the bag into the backseat, mumbling something about my mother.

I dug through the bag in search of the largest pill I could find.

—You're not seriously taking another one? Bettie said.

—I'm not going where I need to go. And I want to go into the fucking stratosphere.

—You don't even know what they are, do you?

I sifted through the bag.

—You can't just combine pills. It could destroy your liver. Or make you delusional, crazy, unpredictable. Or kill you.

—After kicking the hell out of that tree, I said, —I'm beginning to think that losing control, completely losing control, might not be such a bad thing.

—I think that's your problem, she said. —Both of you. You seem like you have to lose control, as you put it, to thrive.

—Tonight I just want to cope. I want to do what we've set out to do and get on with the rest of my life.

—You may freak out to cope, Gummo said, —But it's way more entertaining to do it just for the sake of doing it.

—But the problem isn't the act, Bettie said, —it's the aftermath. Cleaning up the pieces.

—That's why you keep going, Gummo said.

—You don't worry about hitting bottom? Or falling off the edge?

—There is no edge. The line between sanity and madness is an illusion. It's defined solely by culture.

—No such thing, Gummo said, almost speaking over me. —Move closer to the edge and it recedes. You can chase it but you'll never reach it.

—But then so what's the point? Why keep leaping over a cliff if you can't fall off it?

—Life's a farce. Then, to me: —Right? To Bettie: —It's a test. See how far we can go. The only time you do fall is when you give up.

—That's shit.

—What the fuck are you talking about? Gummo said. —I got that from you. Dick.

Silence.

Silence.

Then Gummo giggled.

—My head, it's … hollow.

—Mine, too.

Relaxation washed over me.

A smile cracked my lips.

I couldn't push it away.

Bettie slugged her bourbon and snatched the bag from me.

—And what are we doing? I said.

—Testing your theories.

She swallowed three pills.

—That a girl, Gummo said. —Let's tear this motherfucker down.

We cruised through a trailer park hidden in a wooded area deep in the country. A welcome sign hanging over an iron fence read, 'Autumn Sunset Homes.' But the park's naturally evolved aesthetic was far removed from an autumn sunset.

'Landfill Pointe'—a better name.

A mountain formed from discarded tires and bike frames loomed over an empty lot. Capsized garbage cans stood or lay on cracked or pockmarked concrete. Weeds and grass sprouted from the cracks. Old bicycles and cars—scavenged, probably—littered cul-de-sacs, sidewalks, and lawns. It brought to mind ghettos in third world countries.

But in America, the poor inhabited a third-world country.

Only the well-off lived in a first world.

Everyone else lived in proto-fascist doldrums

We crept down a road parallel to a cluster of trailers, headlights off.

By choice this time.

Bettie pointed out a doll lying on the ground.

—That's creepy, she said. Then: —Why are we here?

—To pay someone a visit.

—A dead man, Gummo said.

My head felt like a Russian nesting doll.

My thoughts expanded, then shrunk and vanished, each decreasing in scope and ambition as its ancestors fell into the graveyard of ideas located somewhere around my prefrontal cortex—in canyons manufactured by my neuroses.

I viewed the world through a half-closed aperture.

My vision blurred.

The edges darkened.

Words mutated as they passed my tongue, as they crawled over my lips. They sounded distant, foreign, as if a phantom lurking behind me had uttered non sequiturs.

Gummo killed the engine and guided the car into a driveway.

—This is the shithole we're looking for, Gummo said.

Time had yellowed the trailer's paint, plywood covered most of its windows, and the porch lay in ruins.

A hole in the trailer's façade looked as though a tree, or maybe a car, had penetrated it.

My stomach twisted and swirled.

Twisted.

Swirled.

—Hey. Gummo snapped his fingers. —You with us?

—Why doesn't it surprise me he lives here?

—Would you expect him to live anywhere else?

To Bettie, I said, —Stay here.

—What's in there?

—I'd listen to him if I were you, Gummo said.

—I took it into consideration.

—Don't fucking start.

—Wherever you go, I go, she said. — Whatever you do, I do. The edge, remember?

—Gummo, reason with her.

—Go, if you want.

—Goddamn it. To Bettie: —Two conditions. You stay by us …

—Deal.

—… and you don't pass judgment.

—What do you mean?

—You'll condemn neither nor Gummo nor me for what we're about to do.

—What are you about to do?

—Add a third condition, Gummo said: —No more questions.

—You're both assholes.

—And you can leave at any time. Just come out to the car and wait for us.

—Once I'm inside, I won't budge.

Gummo smacked my chest. —We found a winner in her, mi amigo.

I stumbled out of the car. It took what felt like an eternity to regain my composure. My legs transformed into hollow tubes. Spongy tubes. My brain felt loose, as if it could fall out at any time.

Every step shifted

shifted

my

equilibrium.

I'd splay my arms and legs and waddle, lopsided.

Gummo suffered from a similar affliction: he performed the lopsided-waddle-dance every few seconds, winding his arms like a child trying to fly.

Those fucking pills.

Why'd we take so many?

Why'd we ...

Bettie was stoned.

Out of her goddamn mind.

Her physiognomy read like the results of a serial killer's polygraph test. Her wonky walk exaggerated her limp. She held out her arms and stiffened her back, but her hips swayed and her spine sort of retracted and protracted with every other step.

I imagined viewing us from above: freaks lumbering forward, spreading the gospel of the freak kingdom.

—Keep it down, Gummo said.

We were laughing.

When did that start?

—When we fall, I said, —we fall hard.

—I'm not feeling so hot, Bettie said.

—Stop chattering your goddamn teeth.

—Stop blinking like that.

—Don't look at me.

—Shut up.

—I should lie down.

—Then go back to the car.

—I said I should, she said. —I didn't say I was going to.

The world spun, transformed. A man with a blurry face ran past me. A woman carried a skull on her hand, like a puppet. Flesh and muscle tissue dripped from the skull. Sounds like an invading army of insects filled the air. Everything froze yet everything moved.

Silence.

Step back.

Ruined plans.

Goddamn.

Can't handle your.

Chattering goddamn teeth.

Gummo cracked his neck as he scaled the porch. Porch. What a stupid word. It hit the ear wrong. Stop chattering your teeth. Don't blink. Shut up. Ruined our plans. Jacob dead. Jacob on fire. Fire. Imagine it. Imagine. He wobbled and watched his feet, watched the planks beneath him. They bowed inward. Inward. Teeth chattering. Smacked face on table. Blood. The fuck you do that for? They're a bunch of freaks. Going to trap us.

He knocked on the door. Each knock sounded like a shotgun blast.

Bang.

Bang.

Bang.

The door shook. Trembled. Chattered teeth. Was it afraid?

Footsteps inside grew.

Louder.

Louder and louder.

You ruined it, goddamn it. Jacob. Jacob dead. Fire consumed him. Imagine it.

The door shook—trembled?—again.

Rodney opened it.

He was clutching a bottle of beer and gazed at us, dead-eyed.

An image plowed into me: I shoved Rodney into the apartment, slammed him to the ground, stomped on his face, his sternum, kicked his balls, his ribs, his throat. He moaned. Chattering teeth. Ruined. Jacob burning. Blood. A beautiful sight.

Another image: cutting off his cock and shoving it into his mouth, singing while he choked to death.

—Well, well, well, he said. —If it ain't the Ghosts of Christmas Past. What're ya'll doing in Butt-Fucked Egypt?

Chewing tobacco fattened his lower lip, alcohol slurred his speech, and the tobacco added a lisp.

—Figured we'd stop by, Gummo said.

—Shit, man, 'sgood to see ya'll. Come on in. He glanced at the sky. —Supposed to storm tonight but I ain't seen shit tell me it's going to.

He pulled his head back into the doorway and spun into the trailer.

Gummo didn't move. He seemed stuck between conflicting thoughts. Do we march forward or retreat?

Then …

At some point he made up his mind: march forward.

Bettie and I followed him.

She puckered her face as our feet hit the carpet. I dismissed the expression with a shrug—but it haunted me.

Was it fear, confusion, disappointment?

The trailer smelled like incense and dirty feet. Trash littered the floor—old pizza boxes, ashes and cigarette butts, empty pop and beer cans and bottles, fishing tackle and plastic grocery bags, and what looked like squirrel pelt.

Gummo and Bettie followed Rodney deeper into the bowels of the trailer, each maneuvering around the garbage—I stood on a doormat atop a rectangle of tiles—while Rodney led the way with little trouble: he simply walked on the garbage.

—So … Rodney fell into the couch and propped his arms on the back, as you might do while hovering near the edge of a swimming pool. —Make yourselves at home.

—I'm good.

—So who's the cutie?

Bettie had watched her feet as she searched for a swath of garbage-free carpet. Her head snapped up when Rodney asked about her.

—Don't talk about me like I'm a fucking piece of meat, she said. —And don't treat me like a child in the next room. If you've got something to say, say it to me.

—Ooh, boy. Rodney clapped. —We got a lively one here, boys. Where in the hell'd ya'll find this girl? To Bettie: —And what the hell you doing with these two, sweetie?

—Are you deaf?

—All right, all right. Settle down. I'm just having some fun. To Gummo: —Long time, no see, Gums. Heard you was in jail. Pigs catch you blowing johns in the alley?

He laughed.

Gummo didn't.

—Admit it, Rodney said, —that shit was funny.

—No, yeah, it was good. Funny stuff. But then you were always funny. To Bettie: —Know who this comedian is?

She shook her head.

—Ram, he said, —why don't you introduce Soupy Sales over here?

—This is Rodney, I said. —Jacob's cousin.

Bettie narrowed her eyes and shook her head.

—I'm your cousin, too.

—You married into his side of the family. Not mine.

—Yeah, well, I'm like family. Might as well be.

I crossed the patch of garbage separating Rodney from me, talking as I walked.

—Family doesn't kill family. And you did kill him, you drunk fuck. Family doesn't crack jokes at his cousin's funeral. Family doesn't proclaim the plans God has for a man lying in a sealed coffin, a fucking coffin you put him in, you worthless piece of shit.

Rodney tried to stand. Gummo nudged him back onto the couch.

—The fuck in Christ's name you assholes think you're …

I clasped Rodney's ears, centered his head.

He glanced to the side.

—Look at me, I said.

He clicked his tongue and glanced to the side again.

—Look. At. Me.

His eyes slid to the center.

—Oh God, Bettie said.

Fear had underscored her words.

—Table's've turned, Rodney said.

I followed Bettie's gaze to a hallway near the back of the trailer. Aaron, Rodney's son, leaned against the wall. Shirtless.

Muscles rippled.

—You know, he said, I half-expected something like this.

He clutched a snub-nosed revolver.

Rodney slammed both hands into my chest.

The force—a boulder toppling over a cliff, a train derailing—knocked me back, and I tripped over the coffee table and hit the ground.

Gummo lunged at Rodney, who launched Gummo back with an uppercut.

I scrambled to my feet and tackled Rodney, driving him into the couch. He grabbed my necklace as he punched me and tore it from my neck.

His fingernails dug into my clavicle.

Blood trickled.

I jabbed the heel of my hand into his face.

Blood squirted from his nose.

I punched him again. Then I pried the necklace—its pendant intact—from his hand and stuffed it into my pocket.

Bettie shouted, —Look out.

For reasons I'll never understand, Aaron had tucked the revolver into his waistline as he charged me.

I pushed my feet into his chest and kicked him away from me.

He fell over a recliner, leaped to his feet, and barreled toward me.

Bettie scooped up a bronze spittoon and assailed Aaron.

He swung at me as Bettie shattered it over his head.

Blood sprayed.

He stumbled.

Bettie spit on him and grabbed the item closest to her, a porcelain elephant, about the size of a head, and swung it. He dodged the blow and grabbed her by the neck.

She called him a fucker.

He slammed her face into the wall.

I punched Rodney, hard, between his nose and ear.

He groaned.

I shoved him away.

Gummo leaped to his feet and pinned Rodney to the floor.

—Sons a bitch.

Rodney threw a punch at me. I kicked him and vaulted over the coffee table and threw my shoulder into Aaron's spine—about six inches above the lumbar region.

We flew forward.

Bettie, who'd turned and crouched and leaned against the wall, spun away from us, narrowly avoiding a three-person collision.

Aaron tried to elbow me but I pushed him into the wall, limiting his movement.

—Piece of shit.

I wrapped my arms around his arms, pinning them to his sides.

He wiggled, squirmed.

Called me a fucker, a motherfucker.

Threatened to gut me.

I rammed my knee into his perineum.

Again and again.

He moaned and threw his head back, and it crashed into the bridge of my nose.

Dazed, I released him and fell to one knee.

He spun and hammered his knee into my jaw and chased it with his fist.

The world dimmed yet its sounds thrived: gasping, heavy breathing, flesh meeting flesh, screams, grunts, footsteps, a crash.

Something slammed into the floor.

I moaned and crawled forward.

And he punched me again.

And again.

Bettie shouted, called someone a cocksucker.

Something shattered.

Glass, maybe.

The aperture expanded and everything slammed into focus, though skewed, as if my eyes had transformed into a .35mm camera with a high shutter:

the world resembled an old film marred by missing frames.

I spun onto my stomach and hopped up. An entity hovered over me, poking my right hand with a million invisible needles. And my head felt like a dollar bill tossed in with the laundry: soft and brittle.

Rodney and Aaron stood over Gummo, who was lying on the floor between the couch and the coffee table.

They kicked him.

They punched and stomped his face and chest.

Bettie sprawled on the floor in front of a fireplace, wide-eyed, dazed.

Blood dribbled from her nose.

She watched me stand. A shock of recognition coated her eyes—she had, it seemed, written me off, or forgot about me altogether.

I pointed to Rodney and Aaron, and spun my wrists and jabbed two fingers in their direction.

She reached for the porcelain elephant.

Wobbling, struggling to overcome my topple-dance, I charged Rodney.

Bettie lunged at Aaron.

She bashed his head with the elephant, shattering the porcelain statue.

Aaron turned, slowly. His eyes mutated, almost atrophied, as they telegraphed bewilderment.

He stumbled forward, slid his palm over the back of his head.

Blood soaked his hand.

He muttered something something and collapsed.

Rodney stopped punching Gummo and glanced at Aaron, who was lying unconscious atop a pile of pizza boxes and cigarette butts.

—You fucking bitch.

I dived at him, shoulder first, and we tumbled over the couch and slammed into a nightstand. A lamp fell on me and shattered. Pain blasted through me, but I didn't care. Instead, I pinned Rodney to the floor and punched and spat on him.

Punched and spat on him.

Punched him.

Kicked him.

And knocked him out.

Silence.

The world stopped spinning.

Silence.

Everything stopped.

Then …

Bettie helped Gummo to his feet.

His left eye was swollen.

Blood painted mosaics on his face.

He leaned into Bettie for support and kicked Aaron, who lay face-down, unflinching.

Gummo kicked him again.

And again.

Again and again.

He muttered something, then yelled something—all unintelligible.

Aaron didn't move.

His ribs expanded and contracted as he breathed, but he didn't try to stand or speak or fight back.

Gummo plucked the snub-nosed revolver from Aaron's waistband.

—Stupid     motherfucker.     Then,     scoffing: —Inbreeding.

—Gummo.

Bettie limped worse than she had a few minutes ago.

I straddled Rodney. He didn't move but I refused to take chances. Knowing the fucker, he probably faked it when I'd knocked him out.

Heavy breathing.

Silence.

Heavy breathing.

Silence.

Gummo opened the cylinder on the revolver, peered into it. He jerked his wrist and snapped the cylinder back into the frame. Bettie broke away from him and limp-walked to me. She grabbed my arm, the one hovering, ready to throw a punch, and lowered it.

—Are you okay? she said.

Gummo stood over Rodney. He spat blood at him. Then he cocked the hammer and pointed the gun at Rodney.

—Gum, I said, shouting as I scrambled to my feet.

He sighted the gun on Rodney's face, somewhere near his eyes.

—We didn't come here for this, I said.

—Jacob was my friend.

—He was my friend, too.

Gummo considered the gun. He tapped the trigger without pulling it.

Bettie stood behind Gummo. She puckered and tensed her face, acting as a Greek chorus, augmenting his performance somehow: she tilted her head, stepped forward, and rested her hand on Gummo's shoulder.

His face melted, resembling a cubist painting: discolored and misshapen.

Blood rushed to his head, darkening it.

He blinked, blinked, blinked.

Then he daubed his eyes with the heel of his hand.

Rodney moved.

Gummo kicked him.

Rodney moaned and propped himself up, onto his elbows, and said, —I wasn't drunk. Then, to me: —If I was drunk, I'd be in jail. Wouldn't I be in jail if I was drunk?

He heaved forward, crying.

—I'd be in jail, for Christ's sake.

Gummo kicked him again.

—It's all about you, isn't it? Then, screaming: —Show me your remorse, motherfucker. You fucking asshole. Show it to me.

Rodney's face reddened.

He cried.

—I see tears, Gummo said. —But I don't sense remorse.

He kicked Rodney.

In the face.

Rodney sighed and fell onto his back.

—Do me a favor, Gummo said, to Bettie. —Find some rope.

She limped into the kitchen and dug through cabinets and drawers and found a length of rope, the too-white vinyl kind, after peeking into a hamper.

Gummo tucked the gun into his waistline, kneeled down, tied Rodney's arms behind his back and his wrists to his feet. Then he tied Aaron's hands and feet.

He glanced at me as he finished the last knot and said, —This isn't fun. It's not fun for me anymore, Ram.



We raced away from the trailer park.

Storm clouds chased us.

The sky darkened.

Silence had invaded the car but I didn't want to define it by speaking, so I allowed it to linger, to envelop the cabin, to drape and suffocate us.

Gummo nursed his wounds in the backseat.

His face resembled a slab of uncooked meat.

Bettie sat in the passenger seat, nursing a bottle of *Jim Beam* as she gazed into the void outside her window.

—It's too quiet, she said.

Silence.

—Cat got your tongue?

Silence.

—Fine. I'll talk. I prefer men who don't talk anyway.

She smiled.

It didn't elicit a response.

—So, she said. And she spoke in a slightly higher pitch, like a comedian winking, so to speak, at an audience. —I must admit: so far tonight has been a hoot. What's next, we going to lynch someone? Burn down City Hall?

Something in her voice, and the things she'd said, jabbed me, and my mind blinked out of existence—I was no longer conscious of consciousness, as Sartre might put it.

It felt hollow when it returned, as if the faculties processing shame had glitched.

—I'm not sure I want to do this anymore, Gummo said. —I don't … I can't …

—Tonight has fucked us. And there's still so much to do. So much before we can even reach that tree. And if we don't reach it by sunrise, then what's the point?

—So what happens if you don't finish it by sunrise? Bettie said.

—That tree has to burn at sunrise.

—Why? What's it symbolize?

—It's Jacob's birthday, Gummo said. —He was born at sunrise.

Something outside distracted Bettie. She leaned forward, nearly kissing the dashboard, and gazed at the horizon.

—Does that lead to the tower? she said, pointing to a road leading to a state park.

—I think so.

—I haven't been here in years, Gummo said.

Fervor had seized the States following Pearl Harbor, and everyone convinced themselves of an impending Japanese invasion, so they erected air defense towers throughout the country.

Even Michigan City, Indiana, far from either ocean, got in on the act.

The tower resembled a cross between a panopticon and the Lighthouse of Alexandria. It sat on a hill overlooking the town. The more or less flat lands of northwestern Indiana allowed anyone standing in the tower to see for miles, and with an open view, you could see in any direction.

A state park now surrounded the tower. Trees and weeds and other growths obscured it. You could see its top from a distance. Otherwise, and especially if you were local, it was easy to overlook.

People more or less forgot about it, and the park surrounding it, which made it the perfect place to catch our breath, so to speak.

We parked in an overgrown clearing, site to a now dismantled playground.

—How'd you know about the tower? Gummo said, to Bettie.

—I've been here before. God, years ago.

—Thought you weren't from around here?

—I never said that.

—You did, I said. —When we first met.

—That's not true. I didn't answer when you asked. Remember?

—Then why the hell were you staying in a hotel? Gummo said.

—I was there to fuck someone I met on the internet. I wasn't about to tell him where I lived. Then she paused and said, —Not that I even know where I live at the moment.

The statement lingered.

No one latched onto it.

Silence.

I got out of the car and stretched and sat on the hood.

Bettie joined me.

Clouds coalesced.

They merged and darkened.

—A storm's coming, she said.

—It'll pass.

—With our luck?

—Stop being such a pessimist, Gummo said, then, singing: —'Always look on the bright side of life.'

He limped to the front of the car, clutching his side.

Bettie slid over. I slid beside her. Gummo climbed the bumper and sat beside me.

He winced and sighed, still clutching his side.

We each disappeared into our heads as we examined the clouds.

Bourbon swam through my veins.

It nauseated me.

The incident back at Rodney's trailer had more or less killed the effect of the pills, and …

Panic seized me.

I patted both pockets, then found the necklace, and twirled the chain, now broken.

The pendant swung back and forth.

Back and forth.

—Ooh, Bettie said. —I like that.

She grabbed the pendant: a clock from Dali's *The Persistence of Memory.*

—It was Jacob's, Gummo said.

The pendant swung.

Swung.

—Tell me about him.

I shook my head.

—Not in the mood.

—What do you want to know? Gummo said.

—I don't know, she said. —I just figure, if I'm taking this trip with you, I should maybe know a little about him.

I followed Gummo's gaze to a rusted pop can.

—What's there to say? I said. —He's rotting in a box and we're trying to figure out what the fuck to do.

—In an existential sense? she said. Then: —I can only offer platitudes, really. But I do advise against murder.

I slapped Gummo's back. —You did the right thing back there, by the way.

He lowered his head, seemed to study something on the bumper.

—Can I ask you something? Bettie said.

Silence.

—Would you have shot him?

Silence.

After a beat, after what felt like hours, Gummo pursed his lips and nodded.

—I'm glad you didn't, Bettie said. —Those guys? They weren't worth it.

Gummo closed his eyes and opened them again.

He bared his teeth, spat.

Then he shook his head.

—You've got a tooth missing, I said.

—What? Where?

—This one. Bettie tapped her front tooth.

He jumped off the hood, clutched his side, and winced. Saying something, too low to hear, he knelt in front of the driver's side mirror and curled his upper lip.

—Goddamn it.

He tore the partial from his mouth and examined the hole.

—That asshole, he said. —These fuckers cost over seventeen hundred dollars.

—We'll get them fixed.

—How?

—I don't mean to be ... Bettie said. —But is that ... she tapped her teeth, pointed to her gum line. —... how you got your nickname?

—I had the name before I lost my teeth.

—Do you mind if I ask how you lost them?

—My douche-bag step-prick.

—You, too? she said. —I'm a member of that club.

—The piece of shit kicked the bucket a few years back. Thankfully.

—Sorry.

—Water under the bridge. He slid his hand in front of him, imitating water flowing through a creek.

—So then what's it mean? The name?

—Chico, Harpo, Groucho, Zeppo, and Gummo.

He counted them on his hand.

Bettie furrowed her eyebrows.

—The Marx Brothers, I said.

—I know who they are. Were. Whatever.

—Geniuses, Gummo said. —I loved them as a kid, watched them religiously. They were the first punks, spread anarchy wherever they went. Their point, I think, was to defy authority, which sat well with me because my step-prick was a royal cocksucker. And so I was all for defying authority. So I'd watch them and fantasize about treating him the way Groucho or Harpo treated an oligarch.

—I remember I once heard something about a fifth brother, Gummo, and that blew my mind. It fascinated me because I'd not heard of him, this mysterious brother. It was shattering in a weird way. I thought I knew everything about the Brothers, then this piece of trivia comes along and ... So I obsessed over him. Wondered why he wasn't in the movies. And I talked about him constantly, speculating on the possible freakishness of his appearance, wondering if that's why he wasn't in their movies. After a while, my mom started calling me Gummo. And it stuck.

—So why wasn't he in the movies? Bettie said.

Gummo tongued the hole in his partials.

Made a sucking sound.

—After the name stuck, I didn't want to know, figured let the mystery remain a mystery, you know? He waved. —I don't know. It's stupid.

—I don't think it's stupid, Bettie said.

I smacked Gummo's back.

—Stupid? I said. —No. Boring? A little. Then to Bettie: —But I'll bet one of us can tell a story that isn't boring.

—Yeah? Who? You?

—Why were you going to fuck a teenager?

—Ram's right, Gummo said. —I'll bet that story's far from boring.

—God. She laughed. —It is twisted, isn't it? But then I think that's why I wanted to do it: it was, I don't know, taboo.

—Is that something you do often? I said. —Break taboos?

—Not until recently, no. But now ... Now I want to know what it's like. To hit bottom. I was almost there once ... She shook her head. —I liked it, to be honest. The darkness. Those awful feelings. Emptiness, dread, despair. So I want to get back there.

—I'm there, I said. —And it's not fun. Stay as far away from it as possible.

—But I have nowhere else to go. I want to hit bottom. I need it, as crazy as that sounds.

—Stick with us, Gummo said, —and you'll get there.

I slid off the hood and stretched my back, arms, and legs.

—I feel like meat tenderized with a sledgehammer.

—I know what you mean, Gummo said.

He stretched, too, touching his elbows behind his back.

—So what's next? Bettie said.

She slapped her hands together and rubbed them, as if applying lotion.

I checked my watch.

—Now we visit a museum.

—A museum?

—A center for the arts, I said.

—A museum.

—A community museum, I said, to Gummo. —Christ, does it matter?

—Museum sounds better.

Bettie laughed.

—Whatever you call it, she said. —Why are we going?

I checked my watch.

—It'll be close, I said. —Go there and come back out here …

I did algebra in my head.

I sucked at algebra.

—Maybe we should skip it.

—You're stoned, Gummo said. —No way are we skipping it.

—We may not have time.

—It's got to be done.

—No, it doesn't.

—Yes, it does.

—Gummo …

—This is bullshit. We've talked about it for how long? Jacob talked about it for how long?

—What has to be done? Bettie said.

—We should just go to the tree before we fuck something else up.

—No. The casino, Rodney, the museum, then the tree. That's the plan. It's always been the plan.

—We blew the casino, so the plan …

—Guys, Bettie said. —Gummo, Ram: talk to me. What's at the museum?

Gummo grinned.

—Tonight, mi amiga, we are going to drop a bombshell on the art world.

—Or watch it explode in our faces, I said.

Gummo buried the pedal.

We were still deep in the country. It'd take at least fifteen minutes to reach the museum.

Talk of it had reenergized Gummo. He had leaped into the car and ordered us inside. We're sticking to the agenda, he'd said.

Our schedule isn't fucked, he'd said.

Sitting around moping or talking isn't an option, he'd said.

We'll take care of business at the museum, he'd said, then focus our efforts on burning that goddamn tree to the motherfucking ground.

Now the world blew by the windows. Cornstalks and tress danced with the wind. Our speed transformed them, and everything else, into tracers and smudges.

Ripples ribbed the clouds.

The clouds.

Darkened.

The remaining continents had drifted and merged, transforming the moon into a hazy dot.

A shadow fell over the earth.

Nearby, a train roared. We were cruising parallel to its tracks. Gummo leaned into the steering wheel and seemed to scrutinize the train.

—Ten to one says I can beat it to the crossing on 300, he said.

—Enticing. But no.

—Twenty to one.

—Not now, Gummo.

—I win, you give me ten dollars. If you win, I'll give you two hundred.

—Like you have two hundred dollars.

—If Ram wins, we'll be dead, Bettie said, laughing.

Gummo laughed, too.

—It's moving way too fast, she said. —I doubt you'd pass it, anyway.

—Want to bet?

—Gummo, goddamn it. No.

—Check this shit.

The engine roared as the car rocketed forward.

We raced toward the crossing, at least four hundred feet away.

The train blasted ahead of us, though not moving as fast as us.

Bettie shouted and punched the door panel. Then she yelled at the train, at the engineer, commanding him—or her—to pick up speed.

Did she actually want a fucking train to hit us?

—You're losing, Gummo said, tittering.

—This ass's taking his sweet time. Doesn't he have a schedule to keep?

—It could be worse, I said. —You could have agreed to sleep with him.

—I think we should revise our bet, Gummo said.

—To hell with that.

Gummo met the lines of the road as it curved.

We careered toward the railroad crossing.

We raced, raced: fifty yards from the crossing.

So did the train: fifty yards, forty yards, thirty.

Bettie stiffened and closed her eyes.

Tension seized me.

Gummo shouted—more of a hoot, really—and stomped the gas pedal.

Twenty yards.

Ten.

The train blasted toward us.

Five.

At least.

The engine growled and the car vibrated as Gummo floored it.

We flew over the railroad crossing, hit an incline and seemed to float.

The train blew its horn and roared behind us, flying past the crossing.

It consumed the field of vision in the back window.

—That's what I'm screaming, Gummo said.

—Shit, Bettie said.

—We can revise our bet. Then, laughing: —
Are you into anal?

—That's … Not with you, I'm not.

I laughed.

—So then what'd I win?

—R-E-S-P-E-C-T.

—Why the hell do I want that?

—Hey, she said, —coming from me that
should mean a lot.

—Such bullshit.

Bettie laughed and drank the bourbon and
passed it to me.

Bettie [*to me*]: Quiet. Thinking?

Silence.

Bettie: About what?

Me: Nothing

The truth: my mind had emptied.

Gummo: Ram prefers to keep to himself.

Bettie: That's not a healthy habit.

Me: What is these days?

Bettie: Tell me what's on your mind and I'll
tell you what's on my mind.

I shook my head.

Bettie: Why are you smiling?

Me: You think you're cute.

Bettie [*feigning astonishment*]: What do you
mean, 'think?'

She curled her lips, then pursed them.

Gummo [*to me*]: I'd do her.

Bettie [*slapping the back of his head*]: I'm
right here, genius.

Gummo: No shit.

Bettie [*to me*]: Now he thinks he's cute.

Gummo: I don't think, love. I know.

Bettie: Sure. Keep telling yourself that. [*beat; to me*] So tell me what's going on in that head of yours.

Me: Nothing. Really.

Bettie: My deal still stands. Tell me and I'll tell you.

Silence.

Bettie: Fine. Since you won't talk, I will.

Gummo: I knew that's what you were getting at. You didn't want Ram to talk as much as you yourself wanted to.

Bettie: [*to Gummo*]: Eat it. [*to me*] I was thinking, a minute ago, before we raced the train, about my ex-boyfriend. The prick ...

I held up my hand.

Me: You know what? I don't want to hear it.

Bettie: Why not?

Me: I'm sure it'll lead somewhere awful, and I don't want to hear about it right now.

Bettie: Wow.

Me: Sorry, but I ...

Bettie: You can be a real asshole.

Gummo laughed.

Bettie: And, trust me, if you think you know where this story's going, you're wrong.

Gummo: Right. You'll tell us he fucked your sister or cousin or mom or whatever while you were at work, and then you'll complain and exclaim, 'all men are assholes.'

Bettie: All men are assholes.

Gummo: I knew it. [*to me*] I should start my own psychic network. [*to her*] That was too obvious.

Bettie: But that's not what I was going to say. I want to …I mean … this asshole …

Me: Please.

Bettie: Fine. Jesus. Prick.

Silence.

Silence.

Bettie: So what, exactly, are we meant to do at this fucking museum?

Me: You'll see when we get there.

Gummo: We're getting rid of a few things that don't belong there.

Bettie: Meaning …?

Gummo: There're paintings there, shit passing for art these days. Bullshit pop culture Andy Warhol-type crap, which we're going to improve.

Me: They're hosting an exhibit there, had it for about a year now. It's a theme, really, that takes up an entire wing. Paintings of corporate logos and products, ideas basically plagiarized from Warhol, images of soup cans and shit like that, without commentary or irony. Jacob and I …

Gummo: And me.

Me: …and Gummo visited the place five, six months ago. And we balked at it, at those god-awful paintings. Quote unquote artists throwing the *Nike* swoop or *Texaco* stars on canvases and calling it art.

Gummo [*scoffing*]: Fuck Warhol.

Me: So Jacob and I …

Gummo: And me. Damn, Ram, why you always leaving me out?

129

Me: ... and Gummo contemplated the logistics of vandalizing them, of turning them into genuine *objets d'art*. [*to Gummo*] And I'm only leaving you out to abbreviate the story.

Gummo: Quit doing it.

Me: Okay.

Gummo: So stop it.

Me: Can I finish the fucking story?

Bettie laughed.

Gummo twirled his wrist, beckoning me to continue.

—Oh, I have your permission? Thanks, I said. Then, to Bettie: —We obsessed over it, tried to figure out how to accomplish it without getting arrested, assuming the museum has a security system.

—It's fairly, obvious, Gummo said, —when you think about it. Or you would assume. But then so Jacob called me one day, out of the blue, and said screw the alarm system. If we get caught, we get caught. We'll call the act our manifesto. He laughed. —Jacob tried to mature, tried to act as though he was sensible, a law abiding citizen, but he was far too twisted to ever settle down.

—So what happened? Bettie said. —Why didn't you do it?

—Dumbass got arrested.

—You say it like I intended to get popped.

—Doesn't matter now, does it?

—Doesn't matter period. Here, take the wheel.

I climbed over the seat and grabbed the steering wheel.

Gummo climbed into the backseat.

Bettie climbed up front and sat beside me.

—Isn't that some shit? Gummo said, and muttered something about foreplay.

He crawled into the trunk, through the backseat, and reemerged with a backpack. Its contents rattled.

He produced a can of spray paint and shook it.

Beads clattered.

He shook it again. Then sprayed the back of my neck.

I threw my arm backward and tried to punch him, but he slid out of reach and sprayed me again.

I tried to punch him and, as I swung my arm, I jerked the wheel, and the car swerved into the opposite lane.

He laughed harder.

Bettie yelled at me, threatened to commandeer the car.

—What are you trying to do? she said.

We were barreling toward a ditch.

I slammed on the brakes, jerked the wheel, and the car spun in the street and stopped.

—You son of a bitch.

I unbuckled my seatbelt and jumped into the backseat. Gummo sprayed me again as he dodged my fist.

A mist wafted toward me. The particles latched onto every gash and wound. They gnawed the meat.

It felt as if he'd thrown sulfuric acid at me.

He cackled and tried to spray me again, but I smacked the can out of his hand, scraping my fist against his knuckles.

—Stop it, Bettie said. —Christ, you're like bipolar children.

I reached for the can of mace in my back pocket.

Shit.

It must have fallen out at Rodney's house.

Gummo exploited the pause by slapping me.

Hard.

I swung at him, but he jerked his head to the side, and I plowed my fist into the seat cushion, clipping his shoulder with my elbow.

—That all you got?

—Keep it up, I said. —And I'll show you what I do have. Now knock it the fuck off.

—No can do, mi amigo.

He slapped me again.

I fumbled as I searched for the paint can on the floorboard.

But I couldn't find it.

I searched again.

And found a bottle of *Jim Beam*.

—The hell you going do with that? He tittered.

I unscrewed the bottle, splashed his face with bourbon.

It hit into his swollen eye—and a gouge on his cheekbone—and he grabbed his face and yelled: —Fucker. Mother …

I opened the door and crawled onto the pavement.

Gummo mimicked me, though less gracefully: he fell onto the pavement and, writhing, wiped the liquor off his face with the bottom of his shirt.

—Motherfuck, he said —That hurt, asshole.

I hardened my face, trying to telegraph hatred and rage.

He backed away from me, pulling his glasses from his pocket. They'd somehow survived.

A minor miracle.

He slapped them on his face and said, —You wouldn't hit a man with glasses, would you?

I punched him.

—The fuck you do that for?

—It can't hurt worse than paint.

—I was goofing around. Christ, go buy a sense of humor already.

Bettie honked the horn. She twisted her wrist, urging us to rejoin her.

—We should get out of the road, she said.

—Come on, stick-in-the-mud, Gummo said. —We'd better get back before mother punishes us. He slid the glasses down his nose. They snapped. —Son of a bitch. You finally killed them.

Bettie had joined me in the backseat.

Gummo drove.

He had fiddled with the radio and finally settled on an AM show broadcast from a desert. Weirdoes and guests regaled the host with tales of ghosts and ghouls, aliens and prophecies.

I had tried to listen as a caller ranted about aliens. They spoke through him, he'd claimed. Dire warnings: they disapproved of our species' behavior.

Then another caller had interpreted Biblical prophesies or something.

Another caller had inquired about orbs and something something.

Blah blah.

Bettie wouldn't stop interrupting them, goddamn it.

She'd talk into my ear without looking at me.

Stories about her ex-boyfriend.

I had tried to listen to the radio—some woman had revealed the supposed identity of the anti-Christ— but Bettie's overweening enthusiasm had pulled my focus from the nonsense spewing from the speakers.

If you judged Bettie's ex-boyfriend solely by her description, he sounded like a bona fide winner.

He was a musician.

A drunk.

A misogynist.

Love had blinded her to the latter, she'd said, and the other two attributes hadn't bothered her—as long as they remained separate. But his mood darkened when he thought about his band while drinking.

Rage ensued.

He'd denounce 'numbfuck' record executives and producers, who, he swore, lacked the vision or the foresight to sign his band.

So he'd drink.

More and more.

And he'd rage against record labels and the morons running them.

More and more.

He'd work himself up, turn into a monster, and beat her.

In the beginning, it had only occurred once or twice. Then he'd renounce liquor and apologize. Profusely.

And she'd take him back.

Then rinse and repeat.

—He's charming, she said. She picked her thumbnail now, glancing at her hands. —You have no idea how charming he can be. He's got this ... And so I'd take him back, even when I knew better. And I always, at least deep down, knew better. And so of course he wouldn't stick to his promise. I fucking knew that. He couldn't or wouldn't go twenty-four hours without drinking, and he couldn't stop thinking about his band when he drank. Yet I still took him back.

Sobriety altered him, she said. He was a wonderful man—or could be: he was sensitive, passionate, compassionate.

But the booze spoiled him.

It turned his brain into a mound of decayed flesh, she said.

When his rage and violence emerged, when he beat her, when he busted her nose or scratched or bruised her, he'd denigrate and humiliate her—and she'd resent him.

She'd loathe him.

She'd fantasize about scarring him, about ripping his eyes out, about skewering his testicles with an icepick.

Then he'd sober up and turn on his charm and she'd forgive him.

Thunder clapped.

It shook the ground as lightning backlit the clouds.

Raindrops. A few fell, then they deluged us.

Rivers flowed down the windshield. Domes beaded on the windows.

About a month ago, roughly around the time Jacob sat in a car racing toward a tree, Bettie's boyfriend had broken her arm and bruised her face. The bruise was massive, she said, shaped almost like Brazil. This time, with such a prominent bruise, she couldn't hide his abuse—from herself or others.

Hatred swelled inside her whenever she glanced at her reflection.

So she left him, and, to her surprise, he left her alone: he didn't sober up, he didn't call her or beg forgiveness.

He simply left her alone.

Licking his wounds, no doubt, she said.

But he contacted her about a week ago. He'd call her, text her, email her, seeking her forgiveness, expressing his love. Begging her to return.

And she ignored him.

He'd leave messages, long messages, in which he expressed sorrow and guilt. He'd cry and swear to stop drinking, to drop out of the band, even.

It'll be different this time, he'd said, I swear it will.

—Now the bastard won't leave me alone. He calls me at work. At home. Leaves messages when I'm not around or refuse to talk to him, begging me to listen. Then, last night, he showed up at my friend's apartment, where I've been staying, and he was drunk, and so he pounded on the door and threatened to stay, to beat the door, until I let him in. We had to call the cops and they made him leave. He's a coward, so of course he didn't put up a fight. Not with a cop. Not with a man. She paused. —But it freaked out my friend, and she pretty much told me to find somewhere else to say, which, I guess, was really why I was at the hotel. She paused again. Then: —I don't trust him anymore. He's a threat now, I think.

Gummo turned off the radio and clicked his tongue. —This guy, he said. —Someone should beat the holy hell out of him.

—Is that something you'd consider?

—Oh, Gummo said. —I'd love to stomp the prick's face. If there's one thing I can't stand, and I mean truly can't stand, it's a cocksucker who beats women.

—Which brings me to the end of my story, Bettie said. —I thought, wondered, really, since we're heading back to town ...

—No, I said.

—But the asshole has to be taught a lesson. Before he hurts someone. Before he hurts me.

—If he keeps acting this way, I said, —that lesson will find him.

—But what if it finds him after he hurts me, after he seriously hurts me?

—I'm sorry, I said, —but not tonight.

Thunder cracked.

Boom.

For a moment I wondered if B-52 bombers were discharging surplus explosives.

Our visibility diminished as the rain thickened.

Gummo turned on the high beams but the headlights transformed the rain into a wall of light.

Lightning illuminated the sky.

Thunder cracked, cracked, a seemingly never-ending cycle of blasts and claps.

Boom.

Boom boom.

Thunder and lightning increased, and the rail fell in waves, as we wound our way back to town.

The streets were empty.

—Feel that? Gummo said. —A dystopian vibe. Fortuna's angry.

Lightning illumined the sky.

Thunder roared.

An explosion to our right jolted me. Gummo yipped.

Sparks and ember rained from a transformer on a nearby telephone pole.

Streetlights flickered. Lights in houses and storefronts darkened.

—It's Fortuna, I said, to Gummo. —You did this, by evoking Her name.

—That's a laugh, coming from you.

—It was sarcasm. Asshole.

—No shit.

—This is the last fucking thing we need.

—It'll stop.

—But it's soaking everything.

—The tree, Bettie said.

We hadn't heard her voice in at least ten minutes.

—That's right, I said. —This shit will drench it.

—Like that'll stop us, Gummo said.

—It will if it keeps coming down like this.

—Keep in mind that we have twelve gallons of gas in the trunk.

—I'd forgotten about that, Bettie said. —I must be used to the smell.

Gummo slowed the car as he tried to see beyond the wall of light and rain.

—Take the back roads, I said. —I don't like being exposed out here. This street's no good.

—Look around. Not a car in sight.

Leaves scattered. They coalesced with the wind and rain. A roar preceded a crashing sound. Near us, maybe twenty feet or so, a lion-sized branch crashed into the ground.

—If it keeps going like this, the cops will probably cruise the streets, warn people to stay off the road, I said.

—I'm surprised they're not out here already, Bettie said.

—Who's to say they're not and we just haven't run into them yet?

—We'd be screwed.

Gummo tittered.

That goddamn noise irritated me more than in the past. An urge to slap him settled in, but I dismissed it.

—We look like we hacked someone up with a butcher knife, he said.

—Plus we have the gun, Bettie said.

—What gun?

—Aaron's.

—Shit. How did I forget about the revolver? —Where is it?

Gummo jabbed a thumb in our direction.

—Back there somewhere.

Bettie and I searched for it. I stuck my fingers into the gaps in the cushions while she dragged her hand along the floorboard.

—Found it, she said.

—Hand it over.

—I'm not touching it.

—It won't bite.

—No. It'll just blow off my fucking fingers.

—You'll be fine as long as you don't touch the trigger.

—Don't care. I'm not touching it.

—Then where is it, goddamn it?

She pointed to a corner obscured by shadows.

I leaned over her and felt for the gun, walking my fingers along the carpet.

Bettie dropped her arm on my back and pushed her pelvis into my shoulder.

She smelled raw, delicious.

I found the gun, wedged partly beneath the driver's seat, and maneuvered it out, paying attention to the placement of my fingers, not wanting to squeeze off a round.

—Got it.

I tried to sit up but Bettie pushed me down and forced me to remain hunched over. Then she rubbed my lower back and snaked her hand around my hip. And she caressed me.

I shut my eyes, steadied my breathing, and thought: fight it.

No.

Don't fight it.

Jacob.

Dead.

Jacob.

Fight it.

She slid her fingers over my crotch, then pulled them toward my knee.

I set the gun aside and pushed the right side of my face into her thigh, near her crotch, and inhaled. She smelled like sex and sweat.

Her pussy smelled sweet and musky.

Her juices flowed.

She dug her palm into my back as she spread her legs. Then she rammed her pelvis into my face again.

I could feel her bush through her panties.

I could practically taste her pussy.

Without thinking, without considering the consequences, if there were any, I sprung up and grabbed her face, vice-like, and kissed her.

She plunged her tongue into my mouth.

—If you're going to have sex, Gummo said, —then I want pictures. Of her, not you.

I broke away from Bettie, half infuriated and half relieved.

Gummo watched us through the rearview mirror.

—Eat shit, I said.

Gummo's eyes flashed to the right. —Looks like you found more than a gun, he said, to Bettie. —I'd be a fucking liar if I told you I'm not at least a little jealous.

Lightning zigzagged across the sky.

Rain and sugar-cube-sized hail pelted the car.

The streets were dark, houses and businesses were dark, everything was dark—except our goddamn headlights. They haloed the rain and hail.

Through slices of light and darkness, I noticed we hadn't slipped onto a backroad.

—I fucking told you to hit the back streets, I said.

—We're almost there.

—We need to steer clear of streets like this, goddamn it.

—Look around. No one's out here.

—Which will make it easier to single us out. There could be a cop parked up the fucking street for all we know.

—Which is why this is so fun. The mystery of it all. The danger.

—Get off this fucking street, I said. —I'm not joking.

—Okay. All right. Don't get your panties in a bunch.

He turned onto the nearest road and maneuvered through a maze of streets.

Not a single streetlight worked.

Not one.

Gummo leaned into the steering wheel as he drove, trying to see beyond the wall of light and rain.

Bettie scooted to me and grabbed my hand.

Part of me wanted to gaze at her. Another part wanted to turn away.

So I didn't react at all.

—Is something wrong? she said, whispering.

—With me?

—Of course not.

—Then what's the problem?

—Women I like usually don't …

My brain crashed.

Silence.

It wouldn't reboot.

Bettie interlaced our fingers.

We turned onto a block with power. Haloes bloomed around streetlights and storefronts. Light spiraled from windows in houses, tattooing yellow and blue rectangles on the lawn.

—Hey, Gummo said, to me. —Got those pills handy?

—I thought you had them.

—I'm fairly certain I gave them back to you.

I searched my pockets, found the bag, and tossed it to him.

—Give me the gun, he said.

—What the fuck for?

—I want it up here.

—Not if you're loading your head with drugs.

—Just give it to me, he said. —Christ, do you have to be a dick about everything?

—I'm not handing over a gun without a good fucking reason.

—I want to hide it in the back of the glove compartment. If we do get pulled over, I sure as hell don't want a cop looking in the window, seeing that goddamn thing staring back at him.

Better reasoning than I had anticipated. So I handed over the gun.

He spun the revolver, Wild West-style.

Bettie and I ducked and dodged as the barrel spun toward and away from us, toward and away from us.

—Knock it off, for fuck's sake, I said.

—Do you think it'd hit anyone? If it went off? He laughed.

—Give it back, I said.

Still laughing, he tossed the gun onto the passenger seat.

—You plus firearms equals me fucking terrified, Bettie said, and she laughed. —It's not comforting. At all.

—Go back to fondling each other.

—You're a fucking idiot, I said.

—Takes one to know one.

—And a child.

—I know you are but what am I?

—I'm going to punch you. To Bettie: —I'm going to hit him. I fucking swear I will.

Gummo tittered.

I wanted to strangle him.

Bettie squeezed my hand until her knuckles whitened. It calmed me somehow. I felt less irritated, and irritable, somehow.

Gummo steered with his knees while he dug through the bag. He plucked out three pills and swallowed them. Then he leaned into the wheel, like Neal Cassady taking Ken Kesey and friends on a field trip.

—Toss the bag back.

—You going to join the party again, Mr. Mopey?

He cackled and tossed the bag back to me.

I dry-swallowed four pills.

Bettie snatched the bag from me, grabbed a few pills, and set them on her tongue, and swallowed.

Then she kissed me. And I kissed her back, hard.

She backed away, wide-eyed and smiling.

I offered a hopefully-cute-and-irresistible smile.

She caressed my cheek. I closed my eyes. Goose bumps grew in her hand's wake.

—Okay, kids, Gummo said. —We're almost there.

Numbness penetrated me.

I opened my eyes, returned to the real world, to the night, to our plans.

I felt hollow.

Empty and dead and alone.

Frowning, Bettie backed away from me. She pulled her arms toward her body, her chest, and dropped them in her lap.

The museum rolled over the horizon, a scaled-down replica of the Parthenon.

—Maybe we should've torched the tree first, I said. —We go in here, we might not come out free people.

—That's the chance we agreed to take.

A possible future flashed in my mind. Police. Darkness. Squad cars flashing red and blue lights. Cops swarming us.

—We should've thought this through.

—Calm down. Christ, Gummo said. —What's got into you?

—We're breaking into a heavily fortified building, for fuck's sake. I should have an EEG, the way I planned this. The tree. Then the museum. Tree. Museum.

—It is risky, Bettie said, —but I think the order's correct. If we burned the tree down first, then this would seem … I don't know … anticlimactic.

—Thank you, Gummo said. —I agree completely. Then, to me: —Drink some more bourbon, pop some pills. Shit, do something.

Gummo stopped across the street and shut off the car. He rested his arm on the back of the seat and offered me a bottle of *Jim Beam*.

—We've come this far, he said. —We'll make it through this.

Hearing those words soothed me somehow.

—Somehow, that doesn't soothe me, I said.

Bettie snatched the bottle from Gummo and chugged. She tapped my shoulder and nudged the bottle toward me. I took it and inhaled what remained.

—If we go to jail, I said, to Gummo. —I'll shank you.

—Not if I get to you first.

He stepped out of the car.

Bettie dropped her hand on my shoulder.

—I think … She paused. Then: —I trust you. I have faith in you.

—The problem with faith is eventually you discover how worthless it is. And you usually discover it the hard way.

She kissed me.

—I wouldn't be so sure of that.

We got out of the car.

Gummo spun and walked backward, smiling. His partials broke loose and dropped onto his lower teeth. He raised them with his tongue and spun around, without acknowledging it'd happened.

Bettie laughed, then barked: —Sorry. I'm so sorry, Gummo.

—Funny. Yeah. That's fucking hysterical.

We crossed the street, walking through elongated scratches of rain.

Thunder clapped.

Then, as if issuing a warning, a bolt of lightning slammed into a transformer on top of a telephone pole twenty feet to our left.

The transformer exploded.

Gummo yelped. Bettie laughed.

Then …

The power and lights in every building, in every street light, vanished.

—See, Gummo said, —I told you Fortuna's on our side.

A shed protruded from the back of the museum, its doors padlocked shut. It concealed an entrance, or exit, long out of commission.

I'd learned about it the previous week, when I'd reconnoitered the grounds.

Gummo plowed his foot into the shed doors. We'd tried to pop the padlock but failed. Now we were stuck watching Gummo play a cop in a shitty movie.

He kicked the door.

Again.

Again.

I ridiculed myself for not bringing bolt cutters.

An honest mistake, Bettie assured me. An oversight.

A gross oversight.

Gummo slammed his foot into the door again.

The door creaked, then cracked, then blew inward, shrieking as it slammed into the inner wall.

—So much for security, he said.

I imagined he pictured himself as an action hero, or some such nonsense when he'd uttered the phrase.

—We're not inside yet.

—Ever the pessimist. Christ.

Inside, the shed smelled like a combination of rotted wood and moldy laundry. Plywood covered French doors, still visible from inside the museum, or center for the arts, where you looked through the glass and encountered surreal mosaics on the back of the plywood.

The only interesting piece in the entire museum.

Or center for the arts.

Whatever.

I swung the backpack onto my shoulder as we stopped in front of the plywood.

—So, Gummo said, to Bettie, —explain yourself. What does Ram have that I don't?

—Dashing good looks, I said.

He mock-laughed.

—Pathos.

—Pathos? What does that even mean?

—Just look at him. Those eyes.

Gummo scrutinized my eyes, studying them as if searching for an image in a cloud.

—They're bloodshot.

—The sadness, she said, —the vulnerability. You don't see it?

His eyes widened. Then he hugged me.

—Oh, you poor thing, he said. —I never noticed before. There, there. Everything'll be all right, my Knight of the Sorrowful Face.

I punched his shoulder.

He tittered.

—Oh, Ram. Don't run away from your feelings.

I fought the urge to laugh, a difficult battle.

But I didn't want to encourage him.

—Go on, Ram, Bettie said, laughing. —Hug him. You know you want to.

—You two are assholes.

—I'm your hero, Gummo said. —Admit it.

I found a paint scraper on the ground and wedged it between the plywood and the wall. Then I instructed Gummo to slip his fingers into the gap when I pulled the scraper back. He leaned into me and stuck his hand into the gap, pulling while I used the scraper as a makeshift crowbar.

—Pull it, goddamn it.

—What the fuck do you think I'm doing?

—Pull harder.

—You do your job, I'll do mine.

—You two … Bettie nudged Gummo aside and slid both hands into the gap.

—On three, I said.

One.

Two.

Bettie pulled, and the plywood snapped and fell away from the wall.

Gummo and I leaped back.

Bettie patted her hands.

—Let me guess, Gummo said, —never send a man to do a woman's job?

—More like 'ask the woman to help.' I'm not incapable of destruction.

—But you're so …

—Think carefully.

—… dainty.

She punched him.

He recoiled.

—If I'm dainty, and you flinched, then what's that make you?

I laughed.

—Hardy har, Gummo said.

I fished a towel from the backpack and wrapped it around my arm.

—What the hell do you think you're doing? he said.

—Face or stomach?

—Don't think about it.

—Face? Or stomach?

—Do it and die.

—Face?

—Give me that goddamn thing. This here is my gig.

—Or stomach?

—I'm not kidding.

—Can't even take a punch.

I unwound the towel, tossed it to him.

—So let me get this straight, Bettie said. —You're ... pointing to me. — ... the idea man, and you ... pointing to Gummo. — ... are the criminal?

—Something like that.

But we ignored him and glanced at the doors. Something blocked them.

—I thought you said it was clear? Bettie said.

A chunk of concrete, like a round table, a marble table, was leaning against the doors. Inside the museum.

Or center for the arts.

Whatever.

So Gummo wrapped the towel around his forearm and slammed his elbow into the door.

The glass shattered.

We ducked and winced, hoping no one was within earshot.

Then he kicked the wood, bifurcating the doors.

We pushed them but they didn't move. Neither did the table.

—Must be made out of marble or something.

—No shit.

—Again, Bettie said. —No respect.

She joined us.

We pushed and kicked the table.

I imagined it weighed five or six hundred pounds.

We pushed harder.

Kicked harder.

Then, on three, we put our combined weight into it.

The sound the table made as it crashed into the floor nearly deafened me.

Bells and horns blasted in my skull.

—Shit.

We froze.

We waited for an alarm to sound, for lights to flash, for something, some sort of esoteric security features, to alert the authorities, to scare us away.

To do something.

Anything.

But no lights flashed.

Darkness.

No sirens sounded.

Silence.

—Maybe the blackout killed the security system, Bettie said.

—You'd figure they'd have a generator.

—I'd have thought it'd be in this shed.

—I'll bet she's right, Gummo said. —Maybe Fortuna's on our side.

—Will you knock it off with that Fortuna shit already?

He held up a finger.

—Don't.

—What's with that anyway? Bettie said.

—A stupid superstition.

—Says you. Then, to Bettie: —I had a vision of Fortuna once. She told me great things were in my future.

—She said it'd rain frogs and fish, I said, —according to this 'vision.'

—No. She said frogs and fish would fall from the sky. And that's when my life would begin. Truly begin. And yours, too.

—What, exactly, do you mean by vision? Bettie said.

—Numbnuts was tripping. Hard.

—The acid had nothing to do with it.

—So experiencing a vision while on hallucinogenic drugs was purely coincidental? I laughed.

—It wasn't the acid.

—What'd She look like? Bettie said.

—Don't encourage him.

—She didn't look like anything. You couldn't see Her, but you felt Her, you know?

—I do, Bettie said. —It's called having a numinous experience.

—Numinous. I like that.

—Can we bracket spiritual and theological contemplations for the moment and get this over with? Before Fortuna gets our asses arrested?

—Don't mock Her.

—Fine. Whatever. Just get inside.

Gummo entered first, Bettie followed, and I trailed her.

As they walked, Bettie leaned near Gummo and said, —I believe you.

—I heard that, I said.

—It wasn't meant to be a secret.

She slowed and walked beside me.

Gummo glanced back at her.

Then at me.

Then at Bettie again.

He shook his head.

—Something on your mind? Bettie said.

—You know, you never answered my question.

—About what?

—Pathos, he said. —That doesn't even make sense.

—I prefer stoic.

—You perform as a stoic, Bettie said. —There's a difference.

—Is it my teeth? Gummo said.

We wandered through an auditorium-sized wing housing American folk art.

—Do my teeth make me unattractive?

—Christ, you've got a one-track mind, I said.

—You guys are like animals. Fighting to win my affection. It's ... cute. She groaned. —I can't believe I just said that. Then, to Gummo: —And to answer your question, no, your teeth do not make you unattractive.

—Then why'd you laugh earlier? Outside?

—I'm genuinely sorry about that, she said. —It caught me off guard. That's it. I'm sorry I laughed.

—Then why him and not me?

Silence.

She gazed at the ceiling.

—He makes me feel ... I don't know ... safe.

—Safe? You got your ass kicked at Rodney's, and he makes you feel safe?

—That's not what I meant.

—Lick those wounds and let's get on with it.

—That's easy for you to say. You got the girl.

—Woman, Bettie said.

—Whatever.

—And he didn't get anything. She grinned. —Not yet.

We examined neo-classical tripe pretentious douches considered art. Statues of David without faces. Romanesque busts of elephants with googly eyes.

Bettie limped.

Each step provoked a cross between a sigh and a grunt.

Her ankle capsized and nearly knocked her to the ground.

I caught her.

She winced as she messaged her ankle.

—Is it broken? Gummo said.

—It's actually made of glass. Real glass. It's a rare condition.

—Everyone's a comedian.

—How long's it been like that?

—Since birth.

—Christ, could you be more obnoxious?

—You want obnoxious? I can show you obnoxious.

—What happened to it? he said. —And no smart ass responses, for fuck's sake.

—Take a wild guess.

—Fine, Gummo said. —Don't tell me. Then, after a beat: —I'm sure you'll tell the Knight of the Sorrowful Face over there.

We stepped into an anteroom leading to a lobby-cum-exhibit hall. Without windows, and still without power, the room was dark. You could see maybe two or three feet in front of you. Beyond that: darkness.

—It smells like paint thinner, Gummo said.

Bettie leaned into me, using me as a crutch—or using her ankle as an excuse to cuddle as we walked: she wrapped her arm around my waist, leaned into me, and hovered her head near my shoulder.

I stole glances, trying to look at her without seeming to pay attention to her.

Her eyes sparkled.

I wanted to dive into them.

I wanted to swim in them.

They could, I suspected, eradicate the dark thoughts, the anger and cynicism, the fear and pessimism and sadness.

—This place is creepy, she said. —It's ... I don't know ... like walking through a graveyard. At night.

I pulled two cans of spray paint from the backpack and tossed one to Gummo. Then I fished my lighter from my pocket and used it as a torch.

The flame projected an orange sphere around us. It cast light—dim, flickering—onto the floor, the walls, the ceiling.

We entered the exhibit hall, our target, and froze.

We froze.

Hatred rotted my brain.

Anger consumed me.

Paint speckled cloth strewn across the floor, a scaffold loomed over buckets encrusted with dried paint, tarps covered kiosks and podiums.

And not a single painting, not a single framed photograph, hung on the fucking walls.

I screamed and shouted.

I kicked a toolbox near me and threw the backpack to the floor.

Gummo spun, scanned the walls.

—What the fuck's going on?

—They were here last week, I said. —The paintings ... None of this shit ... It wasn't ... None of this was here. The paintings were here. Right fucking here.

Gummo clenched the paint can as if it were a stress ball.

He closed his eyes, knelt down, and popped his neck.

Silence.

Silence.

Then he opened his eyes and leaped up and, shouting, yelling, cursing Fortuna, calling Her a cunt, he lobbed the can at the floor.

Paint splattered against us, the floor, the walls.

I checked Bettie for shrapnel. She returned the favor.

That cunt Fortuna, it seemed, had spared us.

For now.

—I don't. Fucking. Believe this, Gummo said. —Goddamn it. Can't anything go right?

His voice shook.

It betrayed emotion.

It revealed, anger, sadness—and it stung me.

I knelt down.

The urge to break something, or to cry, seized me.

—I give up, I said.

Gummo scoffed. —The tree will make up for this. It'll make up for everything.

—Nothing will at this point.

—But we've got to keep going, Bettie said. —We've got to push forward.

—What's the point? It's not going to change anything.

—Nothing we do tonight was supposed to change anything, Gummo said. —Was it?

No.

Probably not.

I didn't know.

—Of course not, I said.

—So what, then? We call it quits? Go home, take a shower? Grab a bite to eat? Watch some fucking television?

—I can't do it. It's too fucking exhausting. I feel drained. Actually drained.

—If you give up now you'll regret it for the rest of your life. And you know it.

—I'll regret it anyway, I said. —I already do.

—The hell you do.

—We've spoiled Jacob's memory, turned it into the punch line of a terrible joke.

—Fuck you, Gummo said.

He slammed the heels of his hands into my chest.

I didn't respond.

I didn't try to fight back.

Bettie grabbed my arms, gazed into my eyes.

—He's right, she said. —Doing this, it's not … It's the point, I think. The meaning. You're doing the right thing. In your own twisted way. She laughed. — If I didn't think so, I wouldn't be here right now.

I tossed my arms into the air and shouted, —Fuck.

Then I bolted into the other wing and plowed into a kiosk. A Romanesque bust toppled over and shattered.

I stomped on the pieces. Tried to disintegrate them. Tried to turn them into powder.

Screaming, I tore a painting off the wall and beat it against a kiosk. The frame snapped. The canvas tore.

—That's it, Gummo said.

He pulled paintings off the walls.

He broke frames.

He shredded canvases.

I threw a bust against the wall and kicked over several podiums.

Everything shattered.

Bettie spray-painted Anarchy symbols on the floor and walls.

—Toss me the bag, Gummo said.

—Heads up.

She tossed it.

—Good arm, he said, and he searched the pockets. —Aha.

He pulled a placard from the backpack and peeled paper from its reverse and stuck the placard to the wall. Then, laughing, he dropped his pants and squatted and dropped a steaming brick on the floor, directly beneath the placard, which read:

## Ruminations on the Exegesis and Futility of Modern Art

—*This piece reflects the shallow pretentiousness of modern art, and those who revere it, specifically works produced in the latter half of the twentieth century and the early years of the twenty-first century, a period in which art passed from the hands of the few to the many, the latter which had developed an obsession and dedication to celebrity and corporate logos and other pop culture paraphernalia they idolized and deemed worthy of worship.*

Bettie cupped her face, laughed, and leaned into me—as if hugging me without using her arms.

Still squatting, Gummo tittered as he fired a few more nuggets at the pile.

I shook a can of spray paint and tagged a nearby wall, quoting my namesake.

### Life is the farce that we all must perform

Gummo pulled up his pants and examined his masterpiece.

—Now, that, he said, —is worthy of admiration.

My phone woke me.

I stayed in bed and stared at the ceiling.

The ringing stopped.

No one called at five in the morning. It was a breach of etiquette, of protocol, of common fucking decency. A person simply didn't do such a thing.

But the mystery, the caller's identity and motive, tormented me. So I threw off the blanket and crawled out of bed and checked the caller ID: Jacob's mother.

We hadn't spoken in over a year, since I'd picked a fight with her new brother-in-law at her wedding reception.

Yet she had called.

Me.

The mystery deepened.

I called her but no one answered.

I lay in bed and stared into the void.

Darkness.

The phone woke me: Jacob's mother again.

—Jacob's dead. She'd issued no warning, no preamble, no 'brace yourself.'

I dropped the phone.

Everything darkened.

All sounds vanished.

An invisible hand grabbed my neck, crushed my windpipe.

My eyes burned.

My stomach writhed.

Tears thickened, then coated, my eyes.

—What do you ... I can't ... What the fuck happened?

—He got in a crash, he ...

She cried.

—Where is he?

—I don't know. I don't ...

—Can I see him?

—No.

—Are you going to see him? Can you see him?

—Yes, she said. —In a couple hours.

—I want to go with you.

She picked me up a few hours later, her eyes red and swollen. Tears bled mascara, which carved black-rimmed canyons down her cheeks.

Frantic, she spoke.

About nothing.

About everything.

Her husband was at work—she couldn't get hold of him—and her sons were God-knows-where, and she was tired because she couldn't sleep. She couldn't sleep because she was sick, a cold, or possibly the flu, and ... and ...

—Thank you, she said. —Thanks for coming. I don't know if I could have done this alone.

The hospital was only about half a mile away but the journey seemed to take hours.

Years, even.

When we found a parking space at the hospital, near the emergency room, though we doubted he was still there, she—Dolores—shut off the car.

But she didn't open her door.

Neither did I.

Phantom noises, remnants of the now silenced engine, filled gaps in my mind. Played tricks with it.

Dolores wiped tears from her eyes.

—Ready?

—I need a cigarette, I think.

—So do I.

I cherished my cigarette, taking small hits. Prolonging and preserving it.

She finished her cigarette and opened the door without stepping outside. She didn't move. Her back to me, she breathed, her rib cage expanding.

I took another hit and tossed the cigarette out the window.

—I just talked to him, she said. —Last night.

—Me, too.

—Why does this have to happen?

I didn't know.

Who has, who does, who will?


We travelled through hallways and spoke to a nurse, then an attendant, then an elderly woman behind a marble desk. She directed us to a series of doors and hallways leading to Jacob—or to the soon-to-spoil meat that once housed the personality we called Jacob.

We took measured steps. The smells, those distinct hospital odors, nauseated me. It smelled the same as all hospitals—bleach and cleaning agents.

My stomach churned.

My throat imploded.

Everything seemed hazy, the world seemed to shatter, my head wobbled, wobbled. I said something something. Dolores asked me to repeat myself. I ignored her. Fuck her.

I ran.

I ran.

But I couldn't find an exit.

I couldn't find a way out.

Trapped.

I felt trapped.

My mind ... I ... Jacob ... lying somewhere in that building.

Dead.

Rotting.

I ...

I found an emergency exit and kicked it open. An alarm sounded. I ignored it and ran outside and lit a cigarette and walked circles around the hospital and ... and ...

A thousand voices roared inside me. They screamed and shouted and yelled. They ordered me to grow up, to act like an adult, like a sensible human-fucking-being. They ordered me to turn and go inside and face his death.

They ordered me to accept and acknowledge his death.

But I suppressed them.

I ignored them.

And I sat on a curb and chain-smoked.

At least half a dozen cigarettes.

Time vanished.

Had I sat there for five minutes?

Or two hours?

I lit another cigarette and built a sundial in the grass.

It didn't work.

—Hey there.

Delores sounded defeated, exhausted.

She sat beside me.

We watched a battalion of ants march across asphalt.

I lit a cigarette. My eighth? Ninth? I'd lost count.

—Can I have one? she said. —I lost mine. Somewhere.

I gave her one.

—They won't let me see him.

—Why the fuck not?

—They said it doesn't work that way, not with his injures. They said it's best if I don't see him. They …

Her sentence hung like a noose above gallows built for me.

—Did they … How was I supposed to frame the question? —What killed him?

—Thermal burns and internal injuries. Massive internal injuries is what they said.

She spoke in a monotone.

The wind blew.

A chill cooled me.

—What the fuck is a thermal burn?

She shook her head.

—So what now? I said.

—We bury him, I guess.

—I mean, what now?

—I should probably see Rodney.

—Rodney?

—He's here.

—Where?

—Room six-sixteen.

—But why is he here?

She told me what had happened.

—Why isn't that cocksucker in jail?

—Because he's injured.

—I hope they fry the son of a bitch.

Silence.

Dolores sat with me for a few more minutes—or hours or days or months. Then she stood and brushed dirt from her backside and ambled toward the hospital.

I watched the ants and imagined running inside, imagined kicking down door after door until I found Jacob.

But then what?

What then?

Burn an image of his charred corpse into my retinas?

Rodney. My thoughts turned to Rodney.

I crushed my cigarette and darted into the hospital. The elevators seemed to take forever, so I took the stairs.

I ran up six flights and slammed into a door leading to a hallway on the sixth floor.

Rodney's floor.

A window at the end of the hall, perpendicular to Rodney's door, framed a portion of the sky, which broadcast the coming of night.

I leaned my head against the glass and glanced at the parking lot, at ants navigating cars, and closed my eyes.

The world stopped spinning.

The universe contracted.

Silence.

Darkness.

Then …

Noise.

I pushed away from the glass and stood in the doorway of room six-sixteen. Rodney was lying in a bed beside a window, eyes closed. A tube ran from his nose to a monitor. Jacob was dead yet Rodney had only suffered a few broken ribs and some lacerations and bruises.

—Hey, I said.

He didn't answer.

He was sleeping.

—I'm going to kill you, I said.

I thought about Jacob, tried not to picture him.

—I should kill you, I said.

Rodney didn't move.

Bandages covered his arms. His hands were the color of uncooked roast.

—Give me one reason, motherfucker, one reason why I shouldn't.

His eyes moved from left to right, right to left, behind his eyelids.

He didn't speak or move or react to me.

I pinched the oxygen tube and leaned into him.

—If it were only this simple, I said.

Then my thoughts, my twisted fucking brain, returned to Jacob. To Jacob. Charred and rotting.

I wanted to talk to him.

To tell him how much he meant to me.

To hug him.

I wanted—needed—to tell him I loved him.

I love you, man.

I backed away from Rodney and drifted into the hallway.

I rode an elevator to the first floor and stumbled through the lobby. Peering down hallways, I wondered where they kept someone like Jacob.

Then I stepped outside and lit a cigarette and cursed myself. My cowardice.

The hospital receded behind me.

I didn't look back.

And I felt like a deserter, like a child running from a shadow, like an adult running from his obligations.

A coward.

I felt like a fucking coward.

Scratch that.

I was one.

We ran to the car.

Rain pelted me, hail stung me. It was cold. Ice cold. The rain fell in waves and pooled in the streets and on the lawns, turning grass and dirt into soup.

Bettie tugged my arm, asked me to slow down. Her ankle hurt, she said. She couldn't keep running.

I matched her speed.

She wrapped her arm around me and rested her head on my shoulder.

—Feel better?

—Do you?

She didn't answer.

—The ankle.

—Hurts. Like a son of a bitch.

Gummo slowed. He looked up and squinted as rain hit his face.

Smiling, he clicked his tongue and turned back around, facing the car.

—What? I said.

—We have all night, really, for you two to just stroll through the rain. Why don't you stop and do a little dance? Maybe make out?

Bettie massaged my bicep.

I broke away from her and joined Gummo at the car. He opened the driver's side door, but Bettie stood between him and the car and said, —Hand over the keys.

—Keep dreaming.

—Why not?

—I drive. He drives. That's the plan.

She pursed her lips and tilted her head and batted her eyes at me.

—Why can't I drive?

I laughed.

And she smiled.

—No, I said.

—Why? Give me one good reason.

—Because few people know how to drive.

—It's because I'm a woman, isn't it?

—I said 'no.'

She pointed to the accordioned hood. —I can't do worse than you.

—She's got you there, Gummo said.

—Fine. You want to drive? Then by all means ...

I swept my arm toward the car.

—Don't worry. I won't wreck it.

—Just get us to the tree, I said.

She snatched the keys from Gummo and hopped into the car. Gummo jumped in the front passenger seat.

And I was left alone in the back.

Bettie drove like an old woman who'd forgot her glasses at home.

I'd told her to stay off the main roads and to watch her speed, but, initially, anyway, she'd buried the pedal and roared down a vacant street.

I'd berated her. And she had relented, slowing the car to twenty-five miles per hour.

Gummo had criticized me as I yelled at Bettie, accusing me of transforming into a prude. When we were younger, he'd said, you'd bury the needle. It didn't matter where we were or what we'd done.

I listened to his stories.

Then I cupped my hand and boxed his ear, telling him to shut his trap.

He twisted in his seat and threatened to punch me, but he lowered his arm after he'd jabbed his elbow into Bettie's neck. She recoiled and threw a hard right at him, clipping his jaw. His head bounced to the side and slapped the window.

—Damn, woman.

—You don't hit me.

—It was a fucking accident.

—You don't. Hit me.

I laughed.

—The fuck's so funny? Gummo said.

—You were right. She is one of us.

—Hardy-har. Then, to Bettie: —Wait'll we hit a stop sign. I'm going to pop your ass.

—I'm not joking, she said.

—Okay, all right. If I give you a dollar will you buy a sense of humor? Then loan it to Ram?

The rain subsided, thinning from a curtain to a screen.

Thunder and lightning continued to roar and illuminate the sky.

Power in most neighborhoods had flickered on and washed the city in light.

Bettie fiddled with the radio while she drove. She'd tired of that weirdo call-in show, so she searched for music, but she didn't find anything worth listening to, so she shut it off.

Jacob haunted me.

Behind a seatbelt in the passenger seat. Rodney. Tires screamed. The car slammed into a tree, propelling Jacob forward. A fire engulfed the undercarriage and the hood.

The fire.

It bred death.

It planted corpses where tombstones grew.

The fire.

The fucking fire.

—Stop, I said.

—What's wrong? Bettie said.

She had turned onto a street in the far corner of town, where the original *cardo* had intersected with the *decumanus* some seventy years ago.

Me: You're going the wrong way. [*To Gummo*] I thought you were navigating.

Gummo: I thought you were.

Bettie: There's something I want to show you.

Gummo [*laughing*]: She's taking us to jail. Told you she's a spy. She's been against us the entire time.

Me: Turn around. We've got to go that way [*pointing behind me*].

Bettie: I will. In a minute.

Me: Now, goddamn it.

Bettie: You've got to see this.

Me: The only thing I've got to see is Jacob's tree.

Bettie: Please.

Gummo [*to me*]: Hold on. [*To Bettie*] I want to hear this.

Bettie: You will. In a minute. It's kind of a surprise, I guess.

Me: Fuck surprises. Turn around.

Bettie: No. You know what? Fuck you. I've been going along with you pricks all night.

Me: And no one forced you …

Bettie: Your asses would be in jail right now if it weren't for me.

Me: And we've repaid you.

Bettie [*laughing*]: How the hell have you repaid me?

Me: By allowing you to tag along.

Bettie [*scoffing*]: You had no choice. [*Beat*] And it's not much of a repayment.

Gummo: She's got you there.

Me [*To Bettie*]: I'm not kidding. Turn this fucking car around. Right. Now.

We cruised down a street still darkened by power outages.

Anger billowed inside me.

I imagined leaping into the front seat and shoving her out the door.

She stopped in front of a house at a cul-de-sac and killed the engine.

Me: What's this?

Bettie: It's a house.

Gummo: No shit, Sherlock.

Bettie: It's Will's.

Gummo: Who the fuck is Will?

Me: Her boyfriend. Goddamn it.

Bettie: Ex. Boyfriend.

Me: Goddamn you. I told you we wanted nothing to do with this.

Gummo: What exactly do you want us to do?

Bettie: Hurt him.

Me: That's not going to happen.

Bettie: Why not? The bastard deserves it. As much as that Rodney prick did. More, even.

Me: Not tonight.

Bettie: If not now, when?

Gummo: Hell hath no fury and all that noise.

Bettie: He beat me.

Gummo: He … what'd he do now?

Bettie: The prick beat me, kicked me, broke my arm, fractured my collarbone, fucked up my ...

Gummo [*quietly*]: Son of a bitch.

Bettie [*to me*]: You're saying that doesn't bother you?

Me: Absolutely not.

Bettie: Yet you won't help me.

Me: Not tonight.

Silence.

Gummo: I'll do it. I'll stomp this asshole's face in. Break every bone in his goddamn body.

Me: What?

Bettie: Really?

Gummo [*to me*]: Let's teach this woman-beater a lesson.

Bettie stared at me.

Gummo stared at her.

We faced each other in a sort of standoff.

Fire ignited his eyes, madness had infected him—an irreversible condition.

Me: Goddamn it. [*After a beat*] Two conditions: You're in and out. Five minutes at the absolute most.

Gummo: That's doable.

Me: And no fighting. Rough him up, threaten him, whatever. But no. Fighting.

Bettie: That's bullshit. No fighting? After what we've done tonight?

Me: Those are the conditions.

Gummo: Then what the hell do you propose we do?

Me: Not we, tough guy. You. I'm sitting this one out.

Bettie knocked on the door.

Gummo leaned against the wall beside the doorjamb.

I popped a cigar into my mouth and stood opposite Gummo.

We flanked Bettie in the doorway, out of view.

She knocked again.

No answer.

No sounds from inside.

—Come on.

She shifted her weight to her uninjured ankle, massaged her temples with her thumb and index finger.

—Doesn't seem like he's home, Gummo said.

—He's here. His car's here.

—That doesn't mean he's here.

—He awake?

—He's a night owl.

She knocked again.

No answer.

No sounds from inside the house.

No sounds at all.

I held my lighter but postponed lighting my cigar, hoping to maintain surprise when Gummo popped into the doorway if the douchebag answered the door.

If.

Bettie knocked again.

Silence.

She grunted.

Gummo leaned his head against the wall and closed his eyes.

Bettie stared at the door while she massaged her temples.

I crossed my arms at my chest and glared at the ground, listening, waiting.

Waiting.

Silence.

—Time's up.

—Wait, Bettie said. —He'll answer.

—He's either not here or he's asleep.

—So, Bettie said. Then, to Gummo: —Kick down the door.

—Let's go, I said.

—He's right, Gummo said. —We came, we tried. This asshole doesn't want to answer …

—I know you hear me. She punched and kicked the door. —Will, you motherfucker. I know you're in there. Answer the fucking door.

A light illuminated the front window.

Then another light flashed on.

Then another.

Footsteps exploded inside.

A raspy baritone sounded, seeming to mutter expletives.

—I regret this already, I said, whispering. Then, to Gummo: —In and out. No fucking around.

—Sshhh, Bettie said. —Shush.

Gummo pressed a fist into an open hand and cracked his knuckles.

A chain rattled.

A lock popped.

The door flung open and a man appeared in the doorway. No taller than 5'6", with a frame small enough to match his stature, he wore an unbuttoned shirt, which revealed a squirrel cage chest, pale skin, and prominent ribs. His hair was matted to his skull and his skin bore a glassy sheen, as if he hadn't showered in days.

When he'd opened the door, he'd shouted, 'what?' tautening his face and furrowing his eyebrows.

His expression had loosened when he saw Bettie.

—Tara, he said. —What in the good Lord's name are you doing?

She crossed her arms, cocked her head, tapped her foot against the landing.

Dried blood had drawn a sort of Rorschach on her face.

—My God.

Will reached out to touch her but Bettie smacked his hand away.

—Is everything all right? he said. —What are you doing here? So late?

Gummo leaned against the house, away from the doorframe, and scrunched his face. If Will had noticed either of us, he didn't acknowledge it. So I turned from him to Gummo and nodded. Gummo smiled.

He leaped in front of the doorway, between Bettie and Will, and shouted, —Boo.

Will screeched and stumbled backward. He laughed, one of those uncomfortable giggles, and said, —What's going ...?

Gummo grabbed Will's shirt, pulling both sides inward. He twisted and knotted the fabric as he pushed Will back into the house.

Bettie followed them inside.

I glanced around the neighborhood—not a person in sight—and closed the door behind me.

Will yelped and tried to break free. But Gummo jerked Will's arm, locked it behind his back.

—The fuck you doing? He tried to twist around. Tried to free himself. —Tara ...?

—Fuck you, Bettie said. —You don't get to ask questions.

Gummo slammed Will's face into the wall. Then he spun him around and slammed his back into the wall.

—Like to hit women?

Silence.

—Huh?

Silence.

—Make you feel big? Give you a hard-on, you worthless piece of shit?

—The bitch is lying. She's filling your head with ...

Gummo smacked him.

—What'd you just call her?

—You're lying, Bettie said. Then, to me: —He's a fucking liar.

She cocked her hand back to punch Will.

I grabbed her arm.

—Let. Me. Go.

She writhed and tried to wiggle away from me, tried to jump away from me, but I wrapped my arms around her, pinned her arms to her chest, and pulled her toward me.

—Gummo will handle this.

—I want a piece of him. Her voice hoarsened, reached a crescendo: —I want a piece of him. I'm not a child. I'm not defenseless. I want to …

—This isn't what we came here for.

—It's not what you came here for. Asshole.

Will said something to Gummo, who slammed Will's face into the wall.

—What the hell …? Will said. —Tara?

—Keep moving, Bettie said. —Give us a reason to break your neck, you piece of shit.

She kicked her feet up and tried to lunge forward, nearly breaking my grip, but I squeezed her arms and lifted her off the ground.

—Let me go, she said, shouting.

—So you like to hit women, Gummo said, to Will. —Why don't you quit being a coward and hit me?

—I ain't done a thing, Will said. —The bitch fooled you. She's manipulating your dumb asses.

—You're a goddamn. Liar, Bettie said.

Gummo squeezed the back of Will's neck. He spun him around, forcing him to look at Bettie.

Will tensed his shoulders, retracted his neck.

—Look her in the eyes, Gummo said, —and call her a liar.

Will smirked.

Gummo flicked Will's ear.

—Look her in the fucking eyes and call her a liar, motherfucker.

—Fuck her. And fuck you, too.

Gummo pulled Will's hair and jerked his head back.

—My patience is thinning.

—She promise each of you a blow job?

Gummo slapped Will.

—That's not a nice thing to say.

Will laughed.

—Now let's try this again, Gummo said. —Look her in the eyes and tell her she's lying.

—I ain't saying a fucking thing. And I don't have to. I ain't pretending to be perfect, but I've made my amends.

—Bullshit.

—Jesus forgives me, Will said. —And that's all that matters.

—Jesus may have forgiven you, Gummo said, —but I haven't. And neither has she. So tell her she's a liar. Or fucking apologize.

—You coward, Bettie said.

She wiggled again, tried to break away from me again, but I managed to hold onto her.

—Where're your balls now? she said. —Come on. Do something. Do something now, you goddamn coward. You worthless chicken hawk.

Will grimaced.

Then ...

He squatted down and leaped into the air and tossed his head back. Gummo jerked his head to the right, avoiding the blow.

As he dodged the collision, Gummo loosened his grip on Will, who exploited the lapse and slunk away from Gummo, kicking him as he launched away from the wall.

Growling, actually fucking growling, he lunged forward, reaching for Bettie.

Bettie mimicked his growl and drove her heel into my shin and elbowed my ribcage.

I tightened my grip on her.

She shouted and screamed, ordering me to release her, ordering me to let her dig her fingernails into Will's eyeballs, pleading with me to let her snap his neck.

Will jabbed Gummo's eye.

Gummo reeled away from him.

—You bitch. Will lunged at Bettie again, reaching for her, snapping his hands, like claws, at her.

She tried to bite his fingers. He withdrew his hand.

Shouting something or other, Will lunged at me.

I spun.

He shouted expletives at Bettie and swung at me without connecting.

Gummo grabbed Will from behind, wove his arms under Will's armpits, around his arms, and interlaced his fingers at the base of Will's skull, forcing him into a full nelson.

Bettie writhed.

She twisted her shoulders and spun her hips.

But I refused to release her.

Will mimicked Bettie: he tried to wiggle, to drop, to free himself.

Red-faced, Gummo stomped the floor and lifted Will and slammed him onto the floor.

Will's face smacked the ground. He gasped and relaxed his body.

Gummo pressed his knee into Will's back and said, —I can be a friendly guy. Hard to believe, I know. But when you hit … when you fucking touch a woman …

—Fuck. You, Will said.

Silence.

Gummo slammed Will's face into the floorboards again. An audible crack replaced the silence. Will sighed, closed his eyes. Blood flowed from his nose and pooled in the cracks in the floor.

Gummo clicked his tongue. He lifted Will's head and said, —Don't go passing out on me.

—The fuck … do you …

—I want to be your friend, Gummo said. —I do. But we can't be friends if you go around beating women. That's a big no-no. A huge one.

Bettie threw her shoulder forward and jerked her arm away from me, breaking my grip.

She flew at Will and Gummo.

I grabbed her arm and pulled her toward me.

—I want to stomp his face with my fucking heel.

—Fuck you, Will said. —Worthless fucking bitch.

—Now now, Gummo said. —That's not very nice. Coming from someone who found Christ and all.

—I should break every bone in your goddamn body, Will said, to Bettie.

—Is that from *Matthew*? *Acts*, maybe?

—Fuck you, you coward, you fucking talentless asshole, Bettie said.

Will's words tore into my flesh and crawled into my brain and sprouted vines.

I should break every bone in your goddamn body.

I should ...

I ...

I should break every bone in your goddamn body.

Break every break every ...

Break every bone in your goddamn body.

The vines spread. They pierced my brain as I fought to contain Bettie.

She writhed.

I held onto her. Refused to release her.

The vines spread, spread.

They replaced every axon.

They filled every synaptic gap.

Bettie shouted and writhed, shouted and writhed.

Vines pierced. Should break every bone break every bone I should break every bone in your goddamn Bettie writhed body.

I flung open my arms.

Bettie hit the floor in a defensive crouch.

She froze, probably unwilling or unable to believe I'd released her.

Then she sprung forward, landed on her right heel, and kicked Will's neck.

She swung her foot into the air, and, in one graceful motion, brought it down on the back of Will's head and twisted her heel into the base of his skull, as if crushing an insect.

Will moaned.

Blood flowed from his nose.

He closed his eyes.

Bettie either didn't notice his reaction or she didn't care. Instead, she kicked his face and stomped his torso with both feet—one after the other—and screamed and cursed him.

A string of saliva hung from her lower lip.

Her eyes reddened and bulged as she screamed.

Gummo stood beside me and we watched Bettie stomp and kick and shout.

—You coward. Piece of shit. No good ...

She kicked Will. She punched him. She spat on him.

I jerked my chin toward her.

Gummo grabbed her and backed her away from Will.

She threw punches and kicks at the air as Gummo pulled her toward me.

—Hey, Gummo said. Bettie ignored him. He shouted, —Hey. Enough.

Tears welled in her eyes.

—You got him, I said. —It's time to go.

I led her to the door.

Gummo lifted Will's head.

Blood had stained the right side of his face.

—You with us?

Will said something or other.

Who knew what?

—Call the cops, Gummo said, —and we'll be back. And we won't be nearly as restrained as we have been. He titled Will's head back and glared into his eyes. —And if I ever catch wind of you hitting another woman, I'll come back here myself and finish what she started.

Bettie's limp worsened as we walked through the door and down the steps.

She leaned into me.

I half-carried her.

Gummo closed the door and sprinted across the lawn and caught up with us as we approached the car.

—Jesus. He laughed. —That was enter-fucking-taining.

I eased Bettie into the backseat.

She gazed at the ground, eyes narrow, teary.

Gummo stood behind me and I turned and grabbed him and forced him into the seat beside Bettie.

—What're you …

—Shut up.

—Don't tell me to shut up.

He tucked his legs behind the passenger seat and glanced at Bettie, seeming to want to say something.

I got in and drove away.

Bettie mumbled something.

—What'd you say?

She said it again.

—That can be scary, Gummo said. —At first.

—Speak up, I said.

—Me or her?

—Her, dipshit.

—I said it felt good, Bettie said.

I watched her through the rearview mirror.

Knots had transformed her hair into an ushanka, mascara trails scarred her cheeks, and tears and dried blood had pooled in her cheeks, chin, and neck.

She met my eyes in the mirror.

And smiled.

A car had turned the corner behind us.

I alternately watched it and Bettie.

It was the first car we'd seen in hours.

Bettie said something and laughed.

The car's headlights grew as it neared us.

It matched our speed yet kept a distance.

Then it flashed its lights at us.


Red and blue lights covered and dyed everything.

—Shit.

—The hell's he pulling us over for?

I punched the steering wheel and said, —Fuck. Fuck fuck fuck. I was speeding.

—You were speeding?

—Fuck.

I punched the steering wheel again.

—What do we do? Bettie said.

—Pull over.

—That's insane, Gummo said. —Floor it.

—That'll ruin us.

—We're already ruined.

—Not necessarily.

—Look at us, Bettie said. —We're covered in blood. We're drunk. You're drunk. I'm with Gummo on this one. We should try to outrun them.

—If we run, this is the end.

—Hit it, Gummo said. —We have no other options.

Headlights silhouetted the squad car.

Its lights flashed.

Red and blue.

Blue and Red.

Inside, a man's silhouette motioned to the side of the road.

—The hell we don't, I said.

I pulled over.

The squad car stopped behind us.

Its interior lights illuminated a single officer, a heavyset man with a crew cut.

I turned off the car and gripped the steering wheel, watching the officer through the mirror.

Bettie and Gummo buckled their seatbelts.

I buckled mine.

—What do we do? Bettie said.

—Just stay calm. Act cool.

—This is crazy, Gummo said. —We should run.

—Shut up, goddamn it.

—What are we going to tell him? Bettie said. —About the blood?

—We hit a deer. In the country.

—That's idiotic, Gummo said.

—Do you have a better idea?

—Yeah. Run.

The squad car rocked and grew three inches as the officer stepped out. He was huge, at least 6'6", at least four hundred pounds, built like one of those wrestlers they'd bill as 'the eighth wonder of the world.'

Clutching a clipboard, he rested his hand on the butt of his pistol and approached us.

I watched him through the mirror, clenching and unclenching my fists.

Through the rearview mirror I saw Bettie's face: drenched in shadows, her pleated eyebrows and forehead telegraphed dread and fear.

She wrapped her hair around her ear and ran her tongue over her teeth, behind her lips. They bulged and relaxed, bulged and relaxed.

—I don't like this, she said.

—This is fucking stupid.

—Just relax. Be cool and relax.

The officer knocked on my window.

I rolled it down.

He glanced into the car, at me.

Then he glanced at Bettie and Gummo.

His eyebrows fluttered.

He glanced at me again and stepped away from the car, grabbing the handle of his gun.

—Get out of the car, he said.

—Is there a …

—Out of the car. Now.

I stepped outside.

Rain drenched me.

The officer flinched and, cupping the clipboard, extended his arm, motioning for me to stop.

So I stopped.

Bettie opened the back door.

The officer jerked his head in her direction, fingering his gun.

—Stay put until I tell you otherwise.

Gummo unfastened his seatbelt and reached over Bettie to close the door. But the officer raised his hand and shouted, —Keep it open. Did I tell you to close it?

Gummo shook his head.

—Huh?

—No, Gummo said. Then: —Sir.

—Then keep it open. And sit up.

Gummo raised his chin and rolled his eyes.

—Is there a problem? the officer said.

Gummo shook his head.

The officer straightened his back and lowered his arm.

—Get out of the car.

Bettie slid toward the door. The officer raised his hand.

—Not you. He pointed to Gummo. —Him.

—How the hell'm I supposed to get out if she doesn't?

—Climb over her. Smart ass.

Gummo mumbled something. 'Bullshit,' maybe.

He climbed over Bettie and stepped onto the street, squinting as rain pelted him.

The officer approached him.

Gummo stiffened his back.

—You been to jail before?

Gummo nodded.

—Then you should know not to act like a cretin in front of an officer of the law.

—Officer, I said. —Look, I know I was speeding …

The officer pointed to the sky.

—I'll be with you in a minute, he said. Then, to Gummo: —Explain to me, as succinctly as possible, why you and your friends look like you've just left a slaughterhouse.

—We …

Without tearing his eyes from Gummo, the officer said, —I didn't ask you, ma'am.

Bettie curled her lips and rolled her eyes and sighed.

—There a problem, missy?

She crossed her arms, shook her head.

—Huh?

—No.

—I'll get to you in a minute, he said. —So keep your trap shut until I do.

She whispered something.

—Excuse me?

—I said, 'okay.'

—Okay what?

—I said okay. Sir. All right?

The officer rested his hand on his waist and studied us, then the car. He walked around to the front and kneeled and examined the bumper.

—This is some serious damage, he said. —What'd you hit?

—A deer.

—Where?

—Out on County Line Road. Back by Five Hundred East.

He gestured to my clothes, my face. —Where'd the blood come from?

—The deer, Gummo said.

—Was I talking to you?

Gummo shrugged.

—There's no blood on the car. No hair. Nothing. How do you explain that?

Gummo closed his eyes and shook his head.

—Hey, the officer said, —I'm talking to you.

—We hit a deer, I said. —A big fucker. And the three of us had to drag it out of the street.

—That the truth?

I nodded.

—So then explain to me why there's no blood on the car.

Words raced through my mind, but each repelled the other, refusing to form a coherent thought.

—Divine intervention, Gummo said.

I closed my eyes.

Fucking moron.

—What'd you say? the officer said.

—It was Fortuna. Divine intervention.

The officer set the clipboard on the hood.

—You've got an attitude problem, he said. —I suppose the time you spent in jail didn't improve your outlook on life.

—I guess not.

The officer followed Gummo's eyes and stopped midway between Gummo and me.

Then he retreated a step.

Something in his eyes, the way he contorted his face …

He darted to the car, pushing Gummo aside, and leaned into the driver's side.

He barked at Bettie, ordering her out of the car.

She slid out of the seat and stood beside me. Gummo joined us and we watched the officer.

My mind raced. I patted my pockets, searching for …

Bettie nudged me. She jerked her eyes to the ground, gesturing to her hand: she was clenching the pill bag.

—Well, well, the officer said. —Looky what we have here.

He backed out of the car …

—Oh, shit, Gummo said.

… pinching the butt of Aaron's revolver.


The officer set the revolver on the hood and reached for something in his utility belt.

He snapped his hand around an empty slot and whipped his eyes toward it.

—Shit.

He glanced at his car and bit his inner cheek. Then he reached for his handcuffs and curled his finger at me.

—Get over here.

Bettie squeezed my forearm, released it.

I glared at Gummo.

He stared at the ground.

Jacob flashed in my mind.

Jacob, dead, lying on a gurney.

Jacob in a car engulfed in flames.

Jacob unconscious.

Jacob dead.

—Over here, the officer said. —Now.

He twisted my wrist and jerked my arm.

—This is bullshit, I said. —The gun's not even mine.

—Shut your mouth. Then: —Whose is it?

—We took it off some asshole, Gummo said, —trying to shoot us.

—Before or after you hit the deer?

He slapped a cuff on my left wrist. My flesh tingled.

—Stop it, Gummo said. —You can't do this. Not tonight.

Not.

Tonight.

Everything slowed.

Slowed.

Gummo yelled at the officer.

Bettie chewed her thumbnail as she slipped the pill bag into her pocket.

The officer's breath warmed the back of my neck.

He tightened the cuff on my left wrist.

It clicked.

Clicked and tightened.

The aperture framing the world shrunk: a tree hovered on the horizon, miles away, standing in a field. The sun broke from the horizon. The tree remained intact.

Jacob's tree.

Free from flames and charcoal-black death.

—No, I said. —No no no no no.

The officer pulled my right wrist near my left wrist.

Images of Jacob's tree, alive and well, had burned into my retinas. They flickered in and out of my mind.

In.

Out.

The officer tried to cuff my right wrist.

He pulled it closer, closer to my left wrist.

Jacob.

Jacob's tree.

Car engulfed in flames.

Jacob's tree.

Engulfed in flames.

I swung my right arm back and buried my elbow in the officer's ribcage. He barreled forward and wrapped his arm around my neck and wrestled me to the ground, shouting, —Stop resisting, as we tumbled forward.

In an attempt to throw him off me, I rocked back and forth, back and forth, but he pinned me down and tried to cuff my right wrist.

I tore my arm away from him and threw my elbow into his face and neck, his sternum and lower ribs.

A pause.

He released my right bicep.

A grunt.

He grabbed my hair and slapped my forehead against the concrete.

Darkness.

Gummo shouted.

Feet slapped the ground.

The officer grunted.

He tensed his muscles and convulsed as he lay on top of me.

Pain tore through my lower back.

Bettie said something.

Someone shouted.

A sound like a hollow thud screamed through the night.

The officer trembled. He tried to stand, to get off me, to rise to his feet, but he fell onto me again.

I threw my shoulder into him and spun onto my side, wiggling out from underneath him.

He got to his knees. I jumped to my feet. Gummo kicked the officer once, twice, three times in the face and chased his foot with a hard right. I rammed my boot into the officer's cheek. Gummo landed another punch.

And the officer fell.

Blood covered his face.

He was breathing but he wasn't moving.

Bettie clenched her forehead and paced back and forth, back and forth.

—Oh god oh god oh god, she said. —This is bad. This is ... oh god oh god oh god.

—We've got to get of here.

—I don't think he's out, Gummo said,

—Who gives a fuck? Bettie said. —We're still going to prison for this.

—No, Gummo said. —If he's conscious he'll call someone.

He kicked the officer again. Then punched him, tearing a hole in the officer's cheek.

The officer's eyes wavered.

Bettie yelled, pleading with Gummo.

The officer whispered something.

Gummo kicked him again.

—Let's go, I said, shouting.

Bettie tried to pull Gummo away from the officer. He pushed her away and kicked the officer again.

In the face.

Again and again.

Bettie ran to me.

—Get in the car, she said. —We've got to fucking move. Stay here and we're dead.

—No, I said. —We have to run.

Gummo stopped kicking the officer.

—The fuck are you talking about? We run, we'll never get to the tree.

—We can't take the car. He would have run the plates. It's on record, goddamn it.

Bettie's eyes widened—it seemed as though, for the first time that night, she realized what madness, and stupidity, she'd embraced.

Gummo kicked the officer again and jumped back, toward me.

—Then what the hell are we supposed to do?

—Run.




Rain pelted us, rainwater soaked our shoes and legs— and we ran.

Up ahead: a forested park, thirty feet away, maybe.

I picked up speed.

Bettie said something.

I glanced at her, over my shoulder: she stopped in the middle of the street and kicked off her heels. Then she bolted toward me, but her limp slowed her, so she walk-ran, jogged, really, as she followed me.

—Ram.

Her limp had worsened.

Behind her, Gummo ran to the squad car after squatting beside the officer. He reached into the car, turned off the lights, and split, throwing something into a nearby drain as he charged in the opposite direction.

I jumped onto a curb and darted over a slope.

The grass was wet and slippery and I nearly fell, but I spread my legs, righted myself, and wobbled as I ran.

I held my forearms in front of my face, elbows touching, as I dove into the foliage. The pine needles punctured and scratched me. I shrugged off the pain and cut through the trees.

The woods were dense, dark.

Insects chirped and screeched and drowned out every noise, except the sounds of rain dripping onto leaves.

Plop.

Plop.

Plop.

I ran until my legs weakened, then I slowed to a fast walk, breathing in shallow gasps. Each breath burned my lungs.

Sweat and rain glued my clothes to my body. I felt the urge to tear off my shirt.

Everything dimmed.

The world hummed.

Nothing made sense.

I spun in a circle, searched for a way out, but I saw only darkness.

Darkness.

Still attached to my wrist, the handcuff smacked my leg as I dropped my arms to my sides. I pulled it and twisted it, trying to slip it over my hand, but the officer had tightened it, and it was stuck.

—Goddamn it.

I pulled the cuffs again.

My wrist burned.

Domes of blood bubbled to the surface, beside the cuff.

Then ...

What was that?

A scream?

Someone screamed.

Bettie screamed.

I tried to distance myself from her. Fuck her. She got us into this mess. She had dragged us off course to teach her ex-fucking-boyfriend a fucking lesson, on this of all nights, and now ...

She screamed again.

Or was she crying?

—Ram. Ram?

Her voice undulated.

Who would save her?

Me?

Fat fucking chance.

She had doomed us.

We had each played our part in dooming us, in ruining the night, our plans, but she had thrown us into a web a cop had circled.

She and Gummo could fuck themselves.

I jogged through the woods, trying to figure out how to reach Jacob's tree, trying to talk myself into stealing a car, to convince myself it was possible to hotwire a car.

But I didn't know anything about cars.

Could you even hotwire a car or was that a bullshit Hollywood convention?

Shit.

Gummo was the car thief, not me.

Silence filled the gaps between Bettie's pleas.

My stomach hollowed.

Images of fire and rain assaulted me.

Jacob stood in front of the tree, glanced down, frowned, as I kneeled at his feet. Head lowered, I cried.

We were alone.

There was no one around to savor the moment.

No one with whom I could relive the night.

Then it hit me—in its darkness, in its solemnity: Jacob and I had shared many adventures, many stories. Now those stories were dead. They'd died with him. And stories were only good and pure and true if you retold them with someone who'd experienced the madness you were describing. None of those stories, none of the experiences I'd shared with Jacob, would live as they had when he and I reminisced, when we remembered events half-forgotten.

We often told stories, when we were drunk or bored, and we'd laugh and snap our fingers and remind the other of an awful or hilarious detail, which is why we tell stories: to remind us, to remember, to understand our sense of self and our place in this universe—not to entertain.

Entertainment could be a side effect of the story, but the telling—the reminding, the understanding—was important.

And someone had to be with me until the end, someone with whom I could later relive this story, someone who'd laugh because he or she was there, someone who'd laugh because he or she—or he and she—had remembered a detail no one else recalled.

The image wavered.

Jacob and the fire blinked out of my mind.

—Ram? Please.

I spun and charged, chasing her voice.

My heart pounded and throbbed.

Pounded and throbbed.

Pine needles cut and scratched me. Blood trickled down my face, neck, and chest. It beaded on my arms.

My body ached.

The booze and drugs had worn off and I felt the sting of every punch and slap I'd endured. It felt as if someone had run me through a paper shredder.

—Don't do this to me. Why are you doing this?

I followed her voice.

Then ...

She was leaning against a tree, rubbing her ankle. Tears streamed down her cheeks. Blood raced down her left cheek, crossing her chin and forming what resembled an upside down anarchy symbol at the base of her neck.

—Can you walk?

—It's killing me.

—What happened to your face?

—A branch ...

I glanced around.

—Where's Gummo?

—I don't ...

—Fucking idiot. Then: —Can you walk?

—I don't know. I think so.

—Lean on me if you have to.

Her ankle bent at an angle and she fell into me.

—Try again.

—I can't. I'm telling you, it's killing me.

—Do you still have the pills?

She tossed the bag to me.

I found two football-shaped pills, assumed they were *Vicodin*, and gave them to her.

—I can't ...

—You have to, I said. —You said it yourself: if we don't get out of here, we're dead.

I dry-swallowed a pill, a purple one.

—See? I said. —Now it's your turn.

She grinned, and that spark, that madness and exhilaration, returned to her face, to her eyes, to the smile blooming on her face.

—Cheers.

She swallowed the pill.

—Now let's go, I said. —I'm sure the police have already realized their boy is missing.

She gasped as she walked, but I held onto her, acting as a human crutch.

—What's your name?

—Ram.

—No. Your name. Your real name.

—It's Ram. Now come on.

Her ankle capsized. I caught her before she could topple over. She bent over and massaged her ankle and muttered something or other.

Something about Will.

—He dropped a monitor on it.

—A computer monitor?

A nuclear warhead detonated in my stomach. It mushroomed across my chest. Its fire and poison blasted into my skull as red drenched the world, and reimagined it.

I swung Bettie over my shoulder, wrapped my arm around her legs, below her ass, and ran.

—Well, hello, she said, laughing. —What the fuck are you doing?

—Getting us to Jacob's tree.

Bettie leaned against a tree, resting in its shadow.

Rain hammered us.

She crossed her arms and buried her nose and mouth in what passed as a neckline—actually, more like a breast line—on her gothic-looking-whatever-she-called-it. She said something about the rain but I couldn't make it out and didn't feel like asking her to repeat herself.

We were standing across the street from Will's house.

Rain rappitty-tap-tapped the tree and concrete.

It rapped the sides and roofs of nearby houses.

Thunder roared.

I'd expected squad cars and SWAT teams and foot soldiers to canvas the neighborhood.

But it was quiet. Not a person in sight.

Only the sounds of rain slapping the ground and flicking leaves filled the night.

—I'm going in, Bettie said.

—No.

—I wasn't asking.

—I'll only be a minute.

—What are you going to do?

—Finish what you and Gummo started.

—Then take me with you.

—I don't want you to see what I'm going to do.

—That's why I want to go.

Her eyes seemed to almost flicker. In them I sensed, more than observed, anticipation and madness. Something sadistic.

My skin crawled.

But those eyes, that darkness, turned me on.

—Christ, I said. —You're a handful, you know that?

—So I've been told.

I picked her up and threw her over my shoulder—she laughed—and ran across the street.

Rain had rendered the street slippery, and I slid across the pavement.

I clutched Bettie's legs and jumped onto the sidewalk, slid into the grass, and bolted up the stairs.

I set Bettie down.

She wobbled and sighed and lifted her leg, hovering her foot above the ground.

—It feels like someone took a chainsaw to my Achilles tendon, she said.

She stood in place and bounced up and down, up and down, as if trying to wake a sleeping limb.

I grabbed both sides of the doorjamb and plowed my foot into the door. It exploded inward, producing a thunder-like crack.

The door hit the wall and bounced back, nearly closing. I pushed it open and ran inside.

Will was sitting on the couch, his head back, eyes closed. A wet towel lay across his forehead.

He flinched when he saw me and fell off the couch. Calling me a 'fucker,' he scrambled to his feet and darted to a doorway leading to another room.

I shoved him back and kicked him onto the couch.

He landed sideways, nearly bounced to the floor, but I stomped his back, preventing him from falling.

—What the fuck do you want from me? he said.

I yanked him off the couch.

He clutched my wrists and wriggled.

Yelling, telling him to shut his mouth, I threw him to the floor and kicked him in the face.

He arched his back and grunted.

I kicked him again.

He grunted again.

Blood flowed from his mouth.

Bettie was standing in the doorway, foot still raised, eyes fixed on Will.

—Make sure he doesn't do anything stupid. I held up a finger. —That goes for you, too: don't do anything stupid.

She limped into the living room and stood over Will.

He watched her, eyebrows furrowed.

She leaned into him, whispered, —That so? and kicked him.

I poked my head into two doorways before I found the kitchen.

I opened drawers, searched them, threw them to the floor. A meat cleaver hit the ground, nearly split my foot. I scooped it up and grabbed the garbage can from the corner and pulled out the bag and tossed it behind me.

Back in the living room: Bettie yelled at Will.

She screamed something but I missed what she'd said.

Will stared at the ceiling and shook his head.

Back and forth.

Back and forth.

—Shut up, Bettie said. —You lie there acting innocent, like the fucking victim. But we know better, don't we? She kicked his ribcage. —You deserve what you got, asshole.

—For God so loved the world that he gave his only son ...

—Knock that shit off. No one buys it.

—... that whoever believes in him should not perish but have eternal life.

—Spewing that bullshit won't help you, Bettie said. —You know it as well as I do.

I set the garbage can in the doorway and ambled to Will.

—So what are you? I said. —Protestant? Catholic? Bettie's eyes dropped to the meat cleaver. —Not that it matters.

—What are you doing? she said, whispering.

Will followed her eyes, then slammed his eyelids shut. —Oh Jesus.

I kicked him.

—Ram?

I slammed the meat cleaver into the floorboard beside Will's head. He screamed and flinched and opened and closed his eyes.

Silence.

He opened them again and looked at the meat cleaver, as if studying it: it was buried in the wood beside his nose.

—Our Father in heaven, hallowed be thy name …

A computer was sitting on a desk in the corner of the room.

—… Your kingdom come, Your will be done …

I lifted the monitor, unplugged it from the tower.

—… on earth as it is in heaven.

—Do it, Bettie said. Then: —No, no, no. Let me.

—Be my guest.

I handed her the monitor.

She raised it over her head and drove it into Will's ankle. It slammed into him as a spade might tear through frozen ground.

Will cried and rolled, writhed and contorted on the floor. He bent his leg and grabbed his ankle. A chunk of bone protruded from his skin.

He cried.

Blood spilled from the wound.

He cried.

—How does that feels, motherfucker? Bettie said. —How. Does. It. Feel?

—Fuck you, he said. —Oh god fuck you fuck fuck you oh god.

Bettie slammed the monitor into his other ankle. The screen and his bone shattered almost in unison.

I kicked him. In the face.

His eyes wavered.

I kicked him again.

He sighed and dropped his arms and passed out.

Bettie dropped the monitor onto Will's back, a smile parting her lips.

—Grab the cleaver, I said. —And the garbage can.

—Why do you want …

—Just get them, for fuck's sake.

Bettie collected the meat cleaver and dropped it into the garbage can as I dug through Will's pockets.

—He has a car, right?

—What are you looking for?

—His keys.

—He keeps them over there.

They were in a candleholder on the computer desk. I scooped them up and tossed them to Bettie.

—Reparations.

I carried the garbage can outside.

Bettie followed me, gasping and sighing and cursing Will as she limped.

—Start the car, I said. —And wait for me.

I ran to the backyard, found the water spigot and amputated a three-foot section of water hose. Water dribbled out and merged with the rain. I left the meat cleaver in the ground, grabbed the hose, and ran to the front of the house.

The engine idled.

Bettie had left the passenger-side door open. She leaned over and watched me.

I tossed the garbage can into the backseat and jumped inside.

—Now let's find Gummo, I said.


Gummo ran to the squad car after he'd kicked the officer. He pushed buttons and twisted knobs until he managed to turn off the lights. Then he pulled the keys from the ignition and threw them into a storm drain as he fled.

He glanced up and down the street, searching for us.

A car appeared about a block away.

A squad car?

It was too dark to tell.

He cut through a nearby yard and scaled a wooden fence and blasted through three or four backyards.

What to do?

What to do?

He bet Will hadn't called the cops. Perhaps he could re-invade Will's house, rough the fucker up again, and take his car.

But as much as that pricked had whined and cried, Will had probably called the police. Gummo was ninety-nine percent certain of it.

So he ran.

Headlights filled gaps between houses.

Fuck.

Was the car roaming the neighborhood?

Gummo's pulse increased.

His heart beat faster, faster, faster, and his fingers twitched, as if each pulse jolted them.

He cut through another yard, ran across an alley, and climbed a tree and hid behind a wall of leaves.

The tree was tall enough to afford a view of my car—and the squad car behind it.

Arrhythmia seized him when another squad car pulled up.

Two officers jumped out, one speaking into a two-way radio.

The other officer ran to his fallen comrade while the first released the radio and held a flashlight at eye-level and searched my car.

The height offered a panoramic view. Two or three blocks away, opposite the police, darkness shrouded a neighborhood.

Still no power.

A reprieve.

Or divine intervention.

Gummo dropped to a lower branch and leaped to the ground. Slipping on the grass, he bounced and wobbled and flew forward, picking up speed while he regained his balance.

Through yards, between houses, across two streets, an alley, and more yards—he ran.

Acid pumped into his veins and corroded his heart.

His chest hurt.

He trembled.

He slipped between two houses and cut through two or three yards, maybe four—he couldn't remember. Lights flashed. Thunder cracked. He darted through alleys and more yards, trying to avoid the street, to steer clear of open areas.

Where to go?

Where the fuck could he go?

Not back to jail.

Fuck that.

His apartment was on the other side of town so it wasn't an option.

A dog growled.

The sound produced a sensation like rippling flesh, a sort of raw fear, something Gummo hadn't experienced. He leaped over a child's toy—a *Big Wheel*—and snagged his pant leg.

He hit the ground, face first.

Hard.

His knee smacked a patch of concrete and searing pain shot up his leg, into his chest, and settled at the base of his skull.

The world dimmed as he fought to breathe.

Pain engulfed his arms and knees.

His head hurt.

Ringing in his ears muffled every other sound.

He pushed himself onto his knees and got to his feet.

His knees burned, almost screamed, as he took a step.

His right wrist spit charged lasers into his forearm and bicep. He hadn't remembered falling on it but the pain told him otherwise.

Holding his wrist against his chest, conscious of the pain, he tried to run, but his knees revolted and forced him to jog.

Jogging, however, consumed too much energy, so he slowed his gait and concentrated on sounds, trying to somehow will the ringing in his ears to go away.

No growling.

No barking.

No sirens or shouting or voices transmitted through receivers.

Silence.

A fleeting urge to find that dog and kick it fluttered through his skull.

As fucked up as things were, he wasn't about to start abusing animals—but, Christ, he wanted to kick that fucker's teeth in.

The storm ebbed: it'd rain, stop, then rain again.

Now rain fell in waves. It flooded the already-soupy grass and dirt, and it turned concrete and asphalt into mirrors reflecting the darkness overhead.

Rain pounced him.

Drenched his clothes.

Gave birth to chills and millions of goosebumps.

He cut through a yard, walked alongside a house, and crossed a darkened street.

He'd developed a limp, and now it worsened with each step.

Sounds of a car, an engine, grew.

His chest and carotid artery thumped, thumped, thumped, drumming the flesh behind his ears.

A squad car patrolled the neighborhood, maybe half a block away.

He spun and cut through another yard and climbed a chain link fence.

His knee buckled at the top of the fence and he flipped over and landed on his back.

Everything hurt now: his back and chest, his head and arms and legs.

He spun onto his stomach and got to his knees.

Then ...

A Rottweiler, tied to a porch, paced a few feet away from him.

Growling, the dog lunged forward.

The rope tautened and yanked the Rottweiler backward.

Gummo fell onto his back when the dog had lunged at him and raised his arms to shield his face.

The Rottweiler bared its teeth and barked and lunged at Gummo again.

The rope pulled it back again.

Gummo flinched and raised his arms again.

Then he stood and ordered the dog to shut its face.

It barked.

Barked.

Gummo hurried through the yard and ran across the alley and into another yard.

He stopped beside a bush and glanced down the street, east and west, searching for cars, scanning for signs of life.

Certain no one was in sight, he limp-jogged through a yard and across the street.

Then …

A car barreled toward him, its headlights off.

Gummo didn't even spot the car until …

… we nearly ran him over.

In a variation on an earlier incident, I clutched the dashboard and shouted, 'look out.'

Bettie was studying the dashboard, trying to figure out how to keep the headlights from flickering on and off.

I yelled at her, told her to fucking stop, goddamn it.

A silhouetted man limped into the street.

She slammed the brakes and pulled the steering wheel to the right. The car squealed and hydroplaned.

The back bumper clipped the man's leg, tossed him to the ground.

Bettie and I tore off our seatbelts and gazed out the back windshield, searching for the man.

For signs of life.

He lay on the street, motionless.

—Oh god oh god oh god, Bettie said. —I didn't mean to I didn't see him what do we do should we check on him should we ...

—Let's assume he's all right.

—We can't ... I don't think we can do that.

The man rose: his body grew in the shadows like a puddle of water rising and morphing into a man.

He lurched forward and pounded the trunk, growling.

Thunder cracked.

Boom.

The man limped around the car, lunged at my door, and flung it open, shouting.

I'd recoiled when the door had opened.

Then I stopped ...

I couldn't move ...

I couldn't believe ...

—Gummo? Bettie said.

I jumped out of the car and hugged him, lifting him off his feet.

—You son of a bitch.

—Put me down, Christ. I set him down. —You fucking hit me.

—I was trying to avoid it, Bettie said.

—Job well done. Then: —Whose car is this?

—Bettie's.

I opened the driver's side door.

—Your license is revoked, I said.

She slid into the passenger side.

—You know what? I didn't want to drive in the first place.

Gummo climbed into the back, beside the garbage can, and muttered a question or two.

I righted the car and turned onto a backstreet and into an alley—and headed for the country.

For Jacob's tree.

The storm annihilated our visibility, transforming the world into a gray-black vacuum.

Gummo again contemplated the garbage can.

—It's for the tree, I said.

—You planning on cleaning up afterward?

—Yes. The world needs more people like us.

—Conscientious, law-abiding citizens, Bettie said.

—Who care about the environment.

—Who let bygones be bygones.

—Who forgive.

—Fuck that noise, I said.

Gummo stretched out and, sighing, massaged his leg from shin to thigh.

—My hip is fucked, he said. —I think my foot's broken.

—I honestly tried to avoid you, Bettie said. —I wasn't trying … But then again, if I'd known it was you …

—Hardy har.

—You know I love you.

—Cute. Then: —Why the fuck were the headlights off?

—Will and I apparently share the same mechanic.

—The cops are everywhere, he said.

—You saw some?

—Half a dozen. At least.

—Shit.

—So maybe driving around without headlights is a bad idea.

—It wasn't by choice.

—Hopefully Will won't wake up. For a while, Bettie said. —And the cops won't know we have his car.

—The way our luck's run? I said. —They've probably already issued an APB.

A car turned onto the road and trailed us. Its headlights shone in the passenger side mirror.

Was it a searchlight?

Its high-beams flooded our car. They haloed the rearview. I couldn't discern the kind of car.

Police or civilian?

Either way, the dick could turn off his high-beams.

Gummo was peering through the back window.

He turned and met my eyes in the mirror.

—Well?

—I can't make the fucker out.

I fastened my seatbelt and advised Bettie and Gummo to do the same.

Bettie took my advice.

Gummo didn't.

I readjusted the mirror, examined the car again.

Bettie raised her eyebrows in upward arches.

I smiled.

—What's that Joplin line? I said. —Freedom means you have nothing to lose?

—… is just another word …, Gummo said.

I rammed the gas pedal into the floorboard.

The propulsion batted Gummo around the backseat. He vanished from the rearview. Then he sat up, muttering something about bananas, and I heard the familiar click as he fastened his seat belt.

—Ram? Bettie said. —Are you high? Drive like this and …

We raced down an empty street.

The car behind us receded. Two dime-sized lights flickered in the rearview mirror.

I turned the corner and tore into an alley, smacking the rear bumper into a light post.

Gummo laughed and yelled. —This is how we do it, bitch. This is how we do it.

Rain bounced off the hood and windshield and rocketed skyward. Some droplets remained to create rainbow-hued splotches on the glass.

We raced down the alley.

And as we neared the end, as I prepared to spin the wheel, to turn onto the street, we hit a speed bump—obscured by leaves and fallen branches—and the car bounced, and we slammed into the street.

I hit the brake and jerked the wheel, spinning the car in a semi-circle.

Bettie yelled.

Gummo tittered.

I cut through a nearby parking lot, squeezed into a vacant spot, and killed the engine.

We spun in our seats, searched for the car.

But it was gone.

—I don't think that was a cop, Gummo said.

We slipped out of town.

The streets were empty, quiet.

We didn't see a single car.

Everyone, it seemed, either slept or avoided the storm.

Out in the country, in the dirt or paved roads, we didn't expect to see another car—and, thankfully, we didn't.

Not one.

Still, I anchored my foot on the pedal and checked the rearview mirror.

Obsessively.

I wouldn't make the same mistake twice.

Another cop wouldn't creep up on us.

Bettie slapped her legs and clenched and unclenched her fists. She snapped and popped her knuckles and clicked her tongue.

—So what are we doing tomorrow? She leaned forward and watched rain fall. —As an encore, I mean.

—We're leaving, Gummo said.

—Yeah. Sure.

—As soon as that tree's in flames, we're out of here, I said.

—Are you joking? Tell me you're joking.

Silence.

—Where are you going?

—Washington State.

—I have an uncle up there, Gummo said.
—Says he can get Ram a job. Then: —I'll sponge off
him.

Bettie screwed her eyes upward.

—You're leaving for a job?

—A good one, I said. —I can buy a house,
maybe afford a decent life.

—But … surely the cops will find you.

Gummo tittered.

—Your car, she said, to me. —They have your
car.

Gummo laughed out loud now.

—We stole it, he said.

—They have fake names. Nothing more.

—But the security cameras. At the casino.

—Faces with no names.

She fell back into her seat and crossed her
arms.

—What am I supposed to do?

—You can sit over there and sulk, I said, —or
you can come with us.

Her eyes sparkled.

—The more the merrier, Gummo said.

Silence.

Her eyes shone.

—So how far is it?

—Washington?

—Yes, Washington, she said. —In kilometers,
not miles.

Silence.

—The tree, she said. To Gummo: —I'm starting to agree with you: he does need a sense of humor.

—The fucker used to have one. But I think he traded it for a Tampon. Used.

—And I shoved it up your ass, I said.

—And I enjoyed every minute of it.

Bettie laughed.

—So how far are we from it?

—Not far.

Silence.

—Fuck, Gummo said. —How the hell are we going to torch it? The gas was in the other car.

I gestured to the garbage can.

—That's plan B, I said.

Picture a Jackson Pollack painting:

Gray paint splattered against a black canvas, distorting it. Layers of gray lines and splotches riddled the canvas, overlapping the black gesso beneath them. The painting exuded energy and chaos, like images inspired by a drug binge. The colors were striking, mesmerizing, violent in their corruption of the once-pure canvas. Someone, it seemed, had mixed acid into the paint, which corroded the frame and ate through parts of the canvas.

Now imagine lifting the painting, enlarging it, and throwing it into the sky, then you'll have an idea of the sight overhead.

Bettie scanned the sky.

—Have you ever seen clouds like that?

—Once.

—When the tornadoes hit, I said.

—That's not funny.

—What's wrong? Gummo said. —Afraid of tornadoes?

—And you're not? Liar.

—The odds of a tornado hitting are close to naught, he said. —Fearing it is nonsense.

—But still … Then: —Forget it.

The clouds shielded the earth from the light of the moon.

Black and gray replaced blue.

Will's car was a disaster: the wires were frayed and the headlights flickered on and off, on and off.

I was, without doubt, an awful car thief.

But no better than Gummo.

—You sure know how to pick them, Gummo said. —About as good as me.

—I was just thinking that. I laughed.

Trees, cornstalks, and woods surrounded us. They shrunk and receded and transformed into flatland as we neared Jacob's tree.

My stomach felt empty. My bones, hollow.

Nausea threatened to flip my stomach inside out.

Jacob flashed into my mind.

On a gurney.

Unconscious in a car as flames engulfed it.

Smiling.

Laughing.

Young and happy.

Smiling.

Fire. Gurney. Dead.

Acres of land surrounded us.

Trees and bushes sprouted up and flew past us.

Rain and wind pounced and shook them.

A bridge grew on the horizon. It arched over the street, connecting two hills.

My fingers twitched.

My head floated.

We were close.

So fucking close.

We were …

Then I saw it.

The tree.

Jacob's tree.

It rolled over the horizon.

I slowed down.

In an open field, about ten yards from the street, near a small lake, an oak tree towered above a row of bushes.

I pulled up near the bridge.

A sensation like swarming insects invaded my stomach and annexed my nerve endings.

I kicked open the door, doubled over, and stared at the ground.

—Are you all right? Bettie massaged my back.

Rain soaked my hair and clothes.

—I think I'm going to throw up.

Gummo unfastened his seatbelt and leaned into the front seat.

—Ram?

I paced in front of the car—back and forth, back and forth—not wanting to look to my left, not wanting to look at Jacob's tree.

Yet everything compelled me to look at it.

I screamed in my head: no, don't look at it.

Then: please, just look.

—Get the garbage can, I said, to Gummo.

He pulled the section of water hose from the can as he approached me.

—A makeshift beer bong?

—Siphon the gas. Funnel it into the garbage can.

—Clever.

—Always the thinker.

—Flip a coin for it?

I hunched over and grabbed my stomach and ran to the back of the car. Saliva coated my mouth. I belched acid, leaned into a ditch beside a concrete slope, and vomited.

Water ran through a ditch below me. It seemed to sigh and groan.

Bettie rubbed my shoulders.

—Are you all right?

I wiped my mouth with the bottom of my shirt.

—Let's get this over with.

Gummo was standing in front of the car, watching me, clutching the hose and garbage can.

—So I assume you're not into the whole coin-flipping thing? Then: —Why the fuck am I always stuck doing shit like this?

—Feel free to collect litter instead.

—Trust me, I'd prefer it to …

—I can't siphon gas. You know that.

Which was true. He, Jacob, and I had tried years earlier. They succeeded. I failed.

—I'll do it, Bettie said. —Let me do it.

—He's done it before.

—And it's awful. I'd rather lick a donkey's taint.

—Then I'll do it, Bettie said.

Gummo threw the garbage can at me …

—The fucking taste stays for days, he said.

… and I threw it back.

He caught it, dropped it, backed away from it.

—Pick it up.

—You're not in charge. This is our plan. Not yours. I call the shots, too.

—Pick it up.

He shook his head.

—You can smell it, you can fucking taste it, for a week, he said.

Bettie stomped past us and scooped up the garbage can and water hose. She pushed past me and strolled to the car. After unscrewing the gas gap and snaking the hose into the tank, she said, —You're worse than children.

She sucked the hose.

She sucked.

Then her eyes bulged.

—Jesus, she said. —It's like trying to suck mud through a straw.

—Give it to me, I said.

She shook her head, sucked the hose again.

—Hand it over.

She yanked the hose from her mouth and, coughing and hacking, spat gas.

—Fuck me, she said.

Gas drained from the hose.

—The can, I said. —Put it in the can.

She lowered the hose into the garbage can. Gas flowed into it.

—Children. She retched and wiped her mouth. —Like bickering toddlers.

Gummo muttered something.

Poo flowed pus?

Bettie flashed a smile.

—What would you do without me?

—Never have a sandwich?

—Hilarious. Pig.

Thunder cracked.

Boom.

It sustained a sort of rhythm as lightning sizzled and illuminated the sky.

Clouds darkened and spun. Clockwise, then counterclockwise.

Thunder roared again.

Boom boom.

Rain fell at an angle, pelting us from the side.

Like an explosion propelling a bullet from its chamber, the thunder exploded as wind slammed into us.

The garbage can fell on its side and slid down the road.

—Get it. Get it, I said.

The wind carried it faster than I could run.

227

I spun on my heel and bolted to the car. Gas spilled from the hose.

The wind snagged the hose and pulled it to the ground.

—Fuck. Mother …

The wind plowed into us.

Bettie fell forward, latched onto the back of the car, and shouted something.

Gummo tried to run to us but the wind prevented him from gaining ground.

He more or less mimed running.

The wind hit again, harder this time. It slammed the doors and rocked the car.

Boom.

On her knees, Bettie leaned into the car and covered her face. Gummo struggled to reach the car: he made it as far as the passenger side door, then he stopped and tried to open it.

The wind slammed it shut.

Again and again.

I grabbed Bettie's arm and pulled her to her feet.

—We've got to hide somewhere, I said, shouting.

—What?

She said something else, but I couldn't make it out. The wind had snatched her voice and carried it away from me.

—We've got to go.

—Where?

Gummo leaned against the car and slid to his knees. He clutched the handle above him with both hands and closed his eyes. The wind punched him, pounced him, rocked him back and forth, back and forth.

I yelled at him.

He didn't hear me.

I yelled again.

The wind and thunder drowned out my voice, so I punched the fender, hard, and screamed his name.

He opened his eyes.

—The bridge, I said, shouting.

He cupped his ear, shook his head.

—Get. To. The. Bridge.

He struggled to stand.

Bettie and I ran to the bridge. Something like a warhead exploded behind us.

—Oh god, Bettie said.

A funnel extruded from the clouds and touched ground, skimming the lake as it cut a path toward us.

Thunder exploded.

The wind threatened to throw us.

The tornado raced toward us.

Toward us.

Bettie yelled something.

Don't let go?

We were holding hands.

I hadn't realized it until that moment.

She led me up a concrete slope beneath the bridge. We ran to the top and hid behind a beam.

Bettie collapsed beside me.

She spun and hugged me and buried her face in my chest.

I hugged her, squeezed her, closed my eyes, thought of her and Gummo and Jacob.

But not before watching frogs and fish fall from the sky.


Wind and thunder enveloped us.

I forced my eyes open and watched as hundreds of frogs and fish rained down on us.

They slammed into the ground. Some flopped. Others bounced away.

Bettie shouted: —What the fuck is happening?

Frogs fell.

Fish fell.

Fucking frogs and fish fell from the motherfucking sky.

Thunder roared as the tornado dragged its tail across the ground.

I clutched Bettie.

The tornado rolled over the bridge: metallic screeches and thumps. It sounded as if someone had dropped a car from a skyscraper.

The cacophony swept over us, through us. The sounds rose to a crescendo. They shook the ground and pounded us, pounded us.

They beat and thrashed us.

Bettie buried her face in my chest. I closed my eyes and held onto her.

Thunder cracked, boom, and added bass to the symphony.

Fish and frogs hit the earth.

I closed my eyes.

Someone screamed.

Bettie?

Gummo?

Me?

The ground beneath us shuddered.

The clouds and sky seemed to crash down around us.

I tried to think.

What to do?

What to do?

Hold on.

Just hold on.

Scream and hold on.

Scream and ...

The tornado dissolved.

Silence.

I opened my eyes.

Light bled through the clouds.

—Is it over?

Blood trickled down Bettie's forehead.

—Are you okay?

She nodded. —You?

—I think so.

She rubbed her forehead, then studied the blood on her hand.

Fish and frogs were strewn from horizon to horizon. They flopped, they croaked, they bounced.

—It must have been from there, I said. Leaves and branches and dead fish floated on the surface of the lake. —The tornado must have displaced the fish and frogs. It must have …

Then it hit me:

—Oh fuck.

I jumped to my feet and slid down the concrete slope.

Bettie chased me.

—What's wrong?

—Gummo.

The storm had destroyed the field beside the bridge. Branches, leaves, and fish and frog corpses cluttered the field and the road. But Gummo wasn't in sight.

The tornado had thrown Will's car across the street. It lay on its side, wrapped around a small tree, which now rested, at an angle, on Jacob's tree.

But Gummo …

—Oh god.

—Gummo. Bettie spun in a circle and shouted his name again: —Gummo?

We ran to the spot where Will's car was parked before the tornado had uprooted it.

It was empty.

The ditch beside the road was empty, too.

The tornado had drained it, probably redistributed the water along with whatever it contained.

Bettie walked up the street, calling Gummo's name. She threw her arms into the air and spun in a circle.

—I don't see him.

I collapsed.

—Ram? I don't ...

I lowered my head and, closing my eyes, dug my hands into a mountain of mud. Rain, or tears, or both, rolled down my nose.

—Look. Look. Bettie tugged my shoulder, laughed, and said, —Ram.

Gummo crawled out of a storm drain in a ditch beside the road.

We ran to him.

—You son of a bitch.

We grabbed his arm and tugged him, pulled him, helped him out of the drain.

He fell onto his ass, dazed.

Blood flowed from a gash on his forehead.

He wiped it with his hand and smeared it along his cheek, above and beneath his eye.

—We thought you were dead, Bettie said.

—Remember what they said when we were young? If you're near a tornado, get to the nearest ditch. Guess school wasn't entirely pointless. He glanced at the storm drain. —You should've seen me. Wiggling around like a goddamn ferret. He tittered. — It'll take more than a fucking tornado to get me out of your hair, mi amigo.

Bettie hugged him.

—You had me worried. Asshole.

—You know you want me.

Bettie punched him, laughing.

—See? he said. —She's acting like a schoolgirl at recess.

We helped him to his feet and climbed the slope.

He pointed to fish and picked up a frog.

—Do you see this shit? Never, and I mean capital-n never, in my craziest, most twisted state, did I ever think I'd see it rain fish and frogs.

—It fucked us, I said.

Will's car lay beside the smaller tree, which leaned against Jacob's tree, which stood about fifteen feet from Gummo, who turned from one to the other and shook his head.

—Fortuna's a cunt.

Tentacles spread in my skull.

They spiraled over my eyeballs, into my nose, mouth, and throat, and strangled me.

—Listen, Bettie said.

—I can't fucking believe this. Gummo kicked a branch. He stomped on it, snapped it in half. —That fucking tree is soaked now. How the fuck are we supposed to torch it?

Thoughts blasted through my mind.

They didn't make sense.

—Do you hear that? Bettie said.

She cocked her head to the side, listening.

—All I hear are those goddamn, motherfucking frogs, Gummo said.

Exactly what I heard: frogs, and thunder.

Bettie ran to the car.

She dropped to her knees, examined something, then, turning to us, shouted, —Gas. Gas is pouring out of it.

—So? Gummo said.

—A branch probably punctured it or …

—So, she said. —Let's burn the car.

I lifted Bettie, spun her, and kissed her, laughing.

—You're brilliant, Gummo said. —Fucking brilliant.

—We do it now, I said. —Before the gas is gone.

Gummo grabbed Bettie's arm, pulled her away from the tree.

—Hope you like fireworks.

I patted my pockets in search of my lighter.

Don't tell me I lost the fucking thing.

But I didn't: it was with Jacob's necklace, snug in my hip pocket.

I held up the necklace and blew on it.

The pendant twisted and spun.

Spun and twisted.

I leaped onto the car and grabbed a branch on Jacob's tree.

It creaked.

—Get on with it already, Gummo said.

I hung the necklace on a twig, watched as the pendant spun clockwise, then counterclockwise, then clockwise again.

Light hit it and splintered and bounced away.

I stopped the pendant from spinning and kissed it.

—Happy birthday, buddy.

Overhead, the clouds had thinned. The rising sun backlit them, transmuting them into mosaics.

Rain sprinkled.

Thunder rumbled.

The storm had moved on, off to terrorize someone else, off to destroy everything in sight, or to make someone's morning miserable.

Or to raise the dead.

I jumped off the car and took out my wallet and dug out a few old receipts and pieces of paper, and twisted them into a wick. After lighting them, I dropped them into the puddle beneath the gas tank. And I backed away.

Flames grew—whoosh—and raced up the stream.

I ran.

I ran.

Then I stopped.

Flames engulfed the car. They broke away from it and raced up the smaller tree.

The fire devoured it and leaped onto Jacob's tree.

Bettie and Gummo met me near the street, and we watched the tree burn.

They yelled and screamed and yipped and yawed.

I didn't say anything.

Instead, I fell to my knees and watched the flames destroy the tree.

And I felt empty.

And I felt satisfied.

But I didn't feel free.

I hadn't exorcized Jacob, I hadn't removed the burden of his death, I hadn't justified his life—and I hadn't given it meaning.

I'd only burned a fucking tree in the middle of nowhere.

Jacob was dead and I was alive.

Jacob was dead and I was alive.

Jacob was dead and I was alive.

Would it sink in if I repeated it enough?

Plumes of coal-black smoke spiraled into the sky as fire consumed the trees and the car.

Rain threatened to extinguish the fire, but the flames were too hot, the smoke too dense.

—Smell that? Gummo inhaled. —Victory.

More rain fell.

But the flames didn't waiver.

They wouldn't or couldn't waiver.

Nothing would dampen the fire.

Nothing would weaken it or put it out.

We'd done it.

We'd done it.

We burned the tree.

Destroyed it.

More rain fell and the wind picked up, but it wouldn't extinguish the flames. It couldn't extinguish the flames. Nothing—not a motherfucking thing—would ever extinguish those flames.

# *Afterword*

I refer to this work as juvenilia. There's no reason to deny it.

I wrote it in late 2003, aged 24, shortly after my cousin had died.

He and I had grown up together.

We were cousins, friends, as close as brothers.

We developed our personalities together.

Our senses of humor.

Our tastes.

He died in a car crash when the driver, drunk, lost control of the car and hit a tree.

The driver died, too.

His brother, in the back seat, survived.

I was in New Mexico at the time, and I couldn't afford to go back to Indiana. I couldn't afford to cross the country to attend his funeral.

And it haunted me.

And it continues to haunt me.

His death crippled me in the early days: I couldn't sleep or eat or drink, and I couldn't form a thought without somehow interjecting him into it—even when he had nothing to do with it.

He haunted me.

His death haunted me.

So I sat down and wrote, and I produced this novel.

My cousin, whom we called Jit—long story—loved dark humor and sarcasm, and he'd developed a fondness for *Fear and Loathing in Las Vegas* after we got baked out of our minds and watched it—he wasn't familiar with Hunter S. Thompson or the book, so the movie was especially memorable to him, I think.

We joked about it for a while.

Talked about skipping out to Vegas and having a *Fear and Loathing* adventure of our own.

He and I weren't sentimental, either, although we loved each other dearly, so when I sat down to write about his death, I didn't want to produce something goopy. I wanted a *Fear and Loathing*-type story, an ode to my cousin, imbued with our opinions and attitudes and twisted senses of humor.

Each act represents a different taste or idea or running joke that he and I shared, yet I wanted the entire book to feel seamless, which is what I more or less produced—I hope.

Initially, I wrote the book to try to come to terms with his death.

I never intended to publish it.

It was simple, sparse, two-dimensional with two-dimensional characters.

It was unsentimental.

Yet I had attached sentimentality to it over the years.

And, over the years, I'd return to it.

I'd try to rewrite it. Try to strengthen it, to develop the characters, to add more depth.

But guilt washed over me whenever I'd attempt it, so I'd put it back where it belonged and leave it alone.

As of this writing, almost twelve years after his death, I thought it was time to revisit it.

I still feel sentimental when I read it, but the distance has offered me a better view of it.

And, to reiterate, it is a work of juvenilia. It is vastly different from the novels and novellas I write now—and I like that. I admire it. I envy the simplicity as I write this, which is nearly impossible for me to do, to mimic the simplicity, as I'm doing now: I'm too used to writing long-winded, tangential, artsy-fartsy novels, I guess.

So I admire the simplicity and the almost cartoonish characters, as well as the fairly tightly focused plot.

It's not a book I could write again, but it's one I'm glad I wrote, and I'm glad I kept it.

And I'm happy to share it with you—something I didn't think I'd ever want to do.

In preparing it for publication, I chose to keep the story and characters intact, exactly as they were when I wrote them. I only made grammatical and syntactical changes, correcting amateurish mistakes by removing adverbs and adjectives, metaphors and similes, and so on—although, obviously, some linger.

It's not the great American novel, but it's a fun one, I think, and I hope you enjoy it.

I'd like to think Jit would have enjoyed it.

But, then again, I wouldn't have had a reason to write it if he were still around.

Goddamn it.
I miss him.

Daulton Dickey
Michigan City, Indiana
27 August 2015